The Old Willow Tree and Other Stories

By

Carl Ewald

The Old Willow-tree

1

There are many kinds of willows and they are so unlike that you would hardly believe them to be relations.

There are some so small and wretched that they creep along the ground. They live on the heath, or high up in the mountains, or in the cold arctic regions. In the winter, they are quite hidden under the snow; in the summer, they just poke up their noses above the tops of the heather.

There are people who shrink from notice because they are so badly off. It is simply stupid to be ashamed of being poor; and the little dwarf-willows are not a bit ashamed. But they know that the soil they grow in is so poor that they can never attain the height of proper trees. If they tried to shoot up and began to carry their heads like their stately cousins the poplars, they would soon learn the difference.

For the poplars are their cousins. They are the stateliest of all the willow-trees and they know it, as any one can see by looking at them with half an eye. You only have to notice the way in which they hold themselves erect to perceive it.

The beech and the oak and the birch and whatever the other trees are called stick out one polite branch on this side and one polite branch on that.

"May I beg you kindly to give me a little bit of sunshine?" says the branch up in the air.

"Can I help you to a little bit of shadow?" says the branch down by the ground.

But the poplars sing a very different tune. With them it is:

"Every branch straight up on high! Close up to the trunk with you! There's nothing to stare at down below! Look above you! Heads up!... March!"

And all the branches strut right up to the sky and the whole tree shoots up, straight and proud as a pikestaff.

It's tiring. But it's elegant. And it pays. For has any one ever seen a smarter tree than one of those real, regular poplars, as stiff as a tin soldier and as tall as a steeple?

And, when the poplars stand along the road, in a long row on either side, you feel very respectful as you walk between them and are not in the least surprised when it appears that the avenue leads right up to a fine country-house.

The dwarf-willows and the poplars belong to the same family. The first are the commonest on the common side, the second are the smartest on the smart side. Between them are a number of other willow-trees. There are some whose leaves are like silver underneath and some whose leaves quiver so mournfully in the warm summer wind that the poets write verses about them. There are some whose branches droop so sorrowfully towards the ground that people plant them on their graves and some whose branches are so tough and flexible that people use them to weave baskets of. There are some out of which you can carve yourself a grand flute, if you know how. And then there are a heap about which there is nothing very remarkable to tell.

The willow-tree in this story was just one of the middling sort. But he had a destiny; and that is how he came to find his way into print.

His destiny began with this, that one of the proud poplars who stood in the avenue leading to the manor-house was blown down in a terrible storm. He snapped right down at his roots; the stump was dug up; and it left a very ugly gap in the middle of the long row of trees. As soon as spring came, therefore, the keeper brought a cutting and stuck it where the old poplar used to stand, stamped down the ground firmly all around it and nodded to it:

"Hurry, now, and shoot up," he said. "I know it's in your blood; and you have only to look down the road to see good examples for you to follow in growing."

Now the man thought it was a poplar he had planted. But it was only a quite ordinary willow-twig, which he had taken by mistake, and, as time passed and the cutting grew up, this came to light.

"What a monster!" said the keeper. "We must pull this up again."

"Let him be, now that he's there," said the squire.

For that happened to be his mood that day.

"Shall we put up with him?" asked the poplars along the road.

They whispered about it for a long time; and, as no one knew how to get rid of him, they agreed to put up with him. After all, he belonged to the family, though not to the smart side of it.

"But let me see you make an effort and grow as straight as you're able," said the poplar who stood nearest to him. "You have found your way into much too fine a company, let me tell you. You would have done better beside a village-pond than in the avenue of a manor. But now the scandal is an accomplished fact and we must hush it up as best we may. The rest of us will shoot up and grow a bit straighter and thinner still; and then we'll hope that the quality will drive past without noticing you."

"I'll do my best," said the willow-tree.

In the fields close by, on a little hillock, stood an oak. On the hillock also grew a charming wild rose. They both heard what the trees of the avenue had said and the oak began to scoff at them:

"Fancy caring to stand out there in the road!" he said. "I suppose you will want to be running up and down next, like those silly men and women? It was unkind and thoughtless of your mother to sow you out there. Trees ought to grow together in a wood, if they are not as handsome and stately as I, who can stand alone."

"My mother didn't sow me at all," said the willow-tree.

"Oh, Lord preserve us!" said the oak. "So your mother didn't sow you at all, didn't she? Perhaps the others weren't sown either? Perhaps you just dropped down from the sky?"

"If you had eyes in your head, you would have seen that the keeper put me here," said the willow. "I am a cutting."

And all along the road the poplars whispered to one another:

"We are cuttings ... cuttings ... cuttings..."

It was a real avenue and a real adventure.

"You managed that very well," said the poplar who stood nearest to the willow-tree. "Only go on as you've begun and we will forgive you for not being as smart as the rest of us."

"I'll do my best," replied the willow-tree.

The oak said nothing. He did not know what cuttings were, and did not want to commit himself or make a blunder. But, later on, in the evening, he whispered to the wild rose-bush:

"What was that rubbish he was talking about cuttings?"

"It's not rubbish at all," said the rose-bush. "It was right enough, what the willow said. I myself came out of a seed, like you, and I didn't see the keeper plant him either, for I happened to be busy with my buds that day. But I have some smart cousins up in the garden at the manor-house. They came out of cuttings. Their scent is so sweet, their colours so bright and their blossoms so rich and full that one simply can't believe it. But they get no seed."

"What next!" said the oak.

"Yes, I, too, would rather be the wild rose I am," said the rose-bush.

Now years passed, as they are bound to pass.

Spring came and summer, autumn and winter. Rain came and snow came, sunshine and storm, good days and bad. The birds flew out of the country and flew back again, the flowers blossomed and withered, the trees burst into leaf and cast their leaves again, when the time came.

The willow-cutting grew and grew quickly, after the manner of the family. He was now quite a tree, with a thick trunk and a top with many branches.

But there was no denying it: he was not a poplar. And his fellow-members of the avenue were greatly displeased with him:

"Isn't it possible for you to grow taller in stature?" asked the nearest poplar. "You ought never to have been here, but, once you've joined the avenue through an accident, I should like to ask you to stretch yourself up a bit."

"I'll do my best," answered the willow-tree.

"I fear your best isn't good enough," said the poplar. "You have no grip at all to keep your branches in with. They hang quite slack on every side, just as if you were a common beech or birch or oak or whatever the ordinary trees are called."

"Do you call me ordinary, you windbag?" said the oak.

The poplar did not mind a jot what the oak said, but went on admonishing the willow-tree:

"You should take example by the squire's wife," he said. "At first she was no better than a common kitchen-maid. She used to scour the pots and make up the fire and stir the milk when it boiled. I used often to see her go down the avenue bare-armed and bare-headed, with a pail in her hand and her skirts tucked back."

"So did we ... so did we ... so did we," whispered the poplars along the avenue.

"Then the squire fell in love with her and made her his wife," said the poplar. "Now she goes in silk, with a train to her dress and ostrich-feathers on her head and gold slippers on her feet and long gloves from Paris on her hands. She looks down from on high: only yesterday she was driving along here in her smart turn-out with the four bays."

"We saw her ... we saw her ... we saw her," whispered the poplars along the avenue.

"She joined the avenue, do you see?" said the poplar. "She learnt to hold herself erect and whisper; and now she whispers and holds herself erect. I think you might profit by her example. After all, you belong to the family, even though you are not one of the real poplars; so it ought to be easier for you than her."

"I'll do my best," said the willow-tree.

But nothing came of it. His branches kept on growing out at the sides and the whole tree was not more than half as tall as the lowest poplars. For the rest, he was quite nice and comfortable-looking, but that's not what counts in the smart world.

And the poplars grew more and more annoyed every day.

They themselves stood stiff and straight and strutted and gave no more shade than their trunks were able to cast. But under the willow there was quite a big shady place.

"He's ruining the whole avenue," said the nearest poplar.

"The whole avenue ... the whole avenue ... the whole avenue," whispered the poplars.

Then, one regular sunny summer's day, the squire came walking along. He took off his hat, wiped the perspiration from his forehead and sat down in the shade of the willow:

"Thank you for your shade, you good Willow-Tree," he said. "Those confounded poplars stand there and strut and don't give as much shade as the back of my hand. I think I'll cut them all down and plant willows in their stead."

For that happened to be his mood that day.

"Did you hear the squire praise me?" said the willow-tree, when he had gone.

"Goodness gracious!" said the nearest poplar. "Did we hear him? It's a perfect scandal! He talked just like a common peasant. But, of course, that comes of marrying a kitchen-maid. It's the truest thing that ever was said, that birds of a feather fly together."

"Birds of a feather fly together ... fly together ... fly together ... together ... together," whispered the poplars all along the avenue.

The oak on the little hillock in the fields twisted his crooked branches with laughter. The wild rose, whose hips were already beginning to turn red, nodded to the willow-tree:

"Every one has his position in life," she said. "We have ours and the smart ones theirs. Now I wouldn't change with anybody."

"Still, one would like to give satisfaction in one's position," said the willow-tree and sighed!

After the warm days came rain and drizzle and wind. The roads became difficult because of the mud and slosh. Only in the avenue did it dry up soon, however hard it had rained. For the poplars gave no shade, so the sun was able to come at once as soon as the rain had ceased. And they gave no shelter either, so the wind came with a rush and dried the puddles.

The squire came driving with his wife. When the carriage reached the place where the willow stood, the wet mud splashed all over her new silk dress.

"Ugh!" she said.

"What's all this nasty mess?" asked the squire.

The keeper, who was sitting on the box beside the coachman, pointed to the willow-tree:

"It's that fellow there," he said. "He was planted by mistake and now he has stood and grown big. He shelters the ground from the wind and shades it from the sun, so there is always a big puddle under him, long after the rest of the avenue is dry."

"Did you ever hear of such a thing?" said the squire. "And the look of him, too! He spoils the whole of the beautiful, stately avenue. See and poll him to-morrow, keeper. Off with the whole of his crown, do you hear?"

For that happened to be his mood that day.

On the next day, they came and sawed the willow-tree down to a man's height. Only the thick naked trunk remained. Not a leaf was left, except five that stood on a little twig down by the ground and really had no business to be there at all. The whole of the splendid crown lay in the ditch. The keeper chopped all the branches into pieces with his axe.

"Will they become cuttings?" asked the willow, disconsolately.

"They will become faggots," replied the keeper and went on chopping to the last stick.

"Then rather let me die at once," said the willow.

"For the present, you will stay where you are, till the winter is past," said the keeper. "When the snow lies thick and smooth all over the roads, you can do good service as a warning-post against the ditch. What will happen afterwards depends upon the squire."

"That was a fine ending to the cutting-farce," said the oak-tree.

"Poor Willow-Tree!" said the wild rose-bush.

"Thank you," said the willow-tree. "I still feel a little stunned. It is no trifle to lose the whole of one's crown. I don't quite know what's to become of me."

"It's a terrible scandal," said the nearest poplar. "A wholly unprecedented family-scandal. If only they would come and take you away altogether, so that you couldn't stand there and disgrace us like a horrible, withered stick!"

"A family-scandal ... a scandal ... a scandal," whispered the poplars along the avenue.

"I don't feel at all withered, oddly enough," said the willow-tree. "I don't know either that I have done anything to be ashamed of. I was set up here and I did my best to fill the position. The squire praised me one day and cut me down another. We must take life as it comes. I shall never be a poplar, but I am one of the family for all that. And a family has other qualities, besides pride. So let us see in a year's time what becomes of me."

"He's speaking like a man," said the wild rose-bush.

The oak-tree said nothing. The poplars whispered in their superior way, but talked no more about the family-scandal.

Now it so happened that the squire and his wife went to Italy and stayed there for a couple of years. And this, in its turn, led to the result that the polled willow was left to stand in peace among the proud poplars. When the master and mistress were away, there was no one who gave a further thought to the stately avenue.

Throughout the winter, the willow stood silent and perplexed. And it is quite natural that a tree should not care to talk when his head is chopped off. But, half-way through March, suddenly one day he fell a-moaning in the most piteous fashion:

"Oh, my head, my head!" he cried.

"Well, I never in all my born days heard the like," said the oak. "Listen to him talking about his head, when all the world can see that it's been chopped off, so that there's nothing but a wretched stump left."

"It's all very well for you to talk," said the willow-tree. "I should like to see you in my place. All my crown is gone, all the big branches and the little twigs, on which the next year's buds used to sit so nicely, each in its axil. But I still have all my roots, all those which I procured when I had a big household and many to provide for. Now the ice on the ground is melting and the sun shining and the roots are sucking and sucking. All the sap is going up through my trunk and rising to my head. And I haven't the slightest use for it.... Oh, oh!... I'm bursting, I'm dying!"

"Poor Willow-Tree!" said the rose-bush.

But round on the other side of the little hillock stood an elder-bush, whom no one talked to, as a rule, and who never put in his oar:

"Just wait and see," he said. "Two or three days will put things right. Only listen to what a poor, but honest elder-bush tells you. Things always end by settling themselves in one way or another."

"Yes, you've experienced a bit of life," said the oak.

"Goodness knows I have!" said the elder. "They have cut me and cropped me and chopped me and slashed at me in every direction. But, every time they curtailed me on one side, I shot out on the other. It will be just like that with the willow-tree. He comes of a tough family too."

"Do you hear that?" said the nearest poplar. "The elder-bush is comparing his family with ours! Let's pretend not to hear him. We'll stand erect and whisper."

"We'll stand erect and whisper ... whisper ... stand erect and whisper," whispered the poplars along the avenue.

"What are those funny little things up in the willow-tree's top?" said the oak. "Just look ... he's swelling, right up there ... it's a regular eruption.... If only we don't catch it!"

"Oh dear no, those are buds!" said the willow-tree. "I can't understand it, but I can feel it. They are real live buds. I am turning green again, I am getting a new crown."

Then came the busiest time of the year, when every one had enough to do minding his own affairs and had no time to think about the poor willow-tree.

The stately poplars and the humble elder got new leaves. The grass shot up green beside the ditch, the corn grew in the fields, the wild rose-bush put forth her dainty leaves, so that the flowers should look their best when they arrived in July. Violets and anemones blossomed and died, daisies and pansies, dandelions and wild chervil and parsley: oh, it was a swarming and a delight on every hand! The birds sang as they had never sung before, the frogs croaked in the marsh, the snake lay on the stone fence, basking his black body in the sun.

The only one who did not join in was the oak. He was distrustful by nature and nothing would persuade him to come out until he saw that all the others were green. Therefore he stood and peered from one to the other and therefore he was the first to discover what was happening to the willow-tree:

"Look! Look!" he cried.

They all looked across and saw that the willow-tree was standing with quite a lot of charming, green, long, lithe twigs, which shot straight up and waved their green and pretty leaves. All the twigs stood in a circle at the top of the polled trunk and were so straight that no poplar need have been ashamed to own them.

"What did I tell you?" said the elder-bush, who stood quite full of dark-green leaves.

"Now I have a crown again," said the willow-tree. "Even though it's not so smart as the old one, it's a crown, as nobody can deny."

"No," said the wild rose. "That's true enough. Besides, one can live very happily without a crown. I have none and never had one and enjoy just as much honour and esteem without it."

"If I may say so, one's crown is only an inconvenience," said the elder-bush. "I had one myself once, but am much more contented since they took it away; and I can shoot my branches as it suits me."

"That's not my way of thinking," said the willow-tree. "I am a tree; and a tree must have a crown. If I had never got a crown, I should certainly have died of sorrow and shame."

"There's poplar-blood in him after all," said the nearest poplar. The others whispered their assent along the avenue.

"Let us now see what happens," said the oak.

6

The summer passed as usual. The sun shone until every living thing prayed for rain. Then it rained until they all cried to Heaven for sunshine.

The willow-tree, however, was not the worst off. He was easily contented by nature. And then he was so greatly pleased with his new crown that he thought he could manage, whatever happened.

Up in the top, in the middle of the wreath of green branches, was a hole which had come when the keeper had chopped off the crown. The hole was not so very small even; and, when it rained, it was full of water, which remained for a good while after the sun had dried the ground again.

One day, a blackbird came flying and sat down up there:

"May I take a drop of water from you, you dear old Willow-Tree?" he asked.

"With the greatest pleasure," said the willow-tree. "By the way, I am not so very old. I have been ill-treated."

"Oh, yes," said the blackbird, "you have been polled! We know all about that."

"Would you be so kind as to wipe your feet?" said the willow-tree. "I only mean that I should not like you to muddy the water if another should come and want a drink. One can never tell, in this drought."

The blackbird scraped his feet clean on a splinter of wood that was there. The splinter broke off and, when the bird flew away, there was quite a little heap of earth left. Next day a swallow came and next a lark and gradually quite a number of birds.

For it soon got about that, at a pinch, there was generally a drop of water to be found in the old polled willow in the avenue. They all left something or other behind them; and, by the autumn, there was so much up there that, one fine day, it collapsed and quite filled up the little hole where the water was.

"You're simply keeping a public-house," said the oak.

"Why shouldn't one be kind to one's fellow-creatures?" said the willow-tree.

It was now autumn. The withered leaves blew up into the willow-tree and lay and rotted. A dragon-fly had lain down to die up there in the latter part of the summer. One of the dandelion's fluffy seeds had fallen just beside her. The winter came and the snow fell on the little spot and lay for its appointed time, exactly as on the ground.

"It is just as though I had quite a piece of the world in my head," said the willow-tree.

"It's not healthy to have too much in one's head," said the oak.

"Once I had a large and glorious crown," said the willow-tree, sadly. "Now I am satisfied and delighted with less. We must take life as it comes."

"That's so," said the wild rose-bush.

"It will be all right," said the elder-bush. "I told you so."

"Horrid vulgar fellow," said the nearest poplar.

"Horrid ... vulgar ... fellow," whispered the poplars along the avenue.

The winter passed and the spring came. Up in the middle of the willow-tree's top peeped a little green sprout.

"Hullo, who are you?" asked the willow-tree.

"I'm just a little dandelion," said the sprout. "I was in mother's head, with a heap of brothers and sisters. Each of us had a little parachute. 'Fly away now, darlings,' said mother. 'The farther away you go, the better. I can do no more for you than I have done; and I won't deny that I am a little concerned about all the children that I have brought into the world. But that can't be helped either; and I hope you will find a spot where an honest dandelion can shift for herself.'"

"Yes, that's just how a little flower-mother talks," said the wild rose-bush.

"What then?" asked the willow-tree.

"Then there came a gust of wind," said the dandelion. "We all flew up into the air together, carried by our parachutes. What became of the others I have no idea; but I remember it began to rain and then I was flung down here. Of course, I thought that, when I had dried, I could fly on again. But not a bit of it, for my parachute was smashed. So I had to stay where I was. To my great surprise, I saw that I was lying on earth. Gradually more earth came, in which I lay hidden all the winter; and now I have sprouted. That's the whole story."

"It's quite a romance," said the wild rose-bush.

"Very likely," said the dandelion. "But what's going to happen to me in the future? Honestly speaking, I would give a good deal to be down in the earth again."

"I'll do all I can for you," said the willow-tree. "I have known adversity myself; and it is a great honour and pleasure for me to have you growing in my poor head."

"Very many thanks for your kindness," said the dandelion. "There's really not so much of it in the world that one shouldn't appreciate it when one meets with it. But, when all is said and done, it's ability that tells; and I fear that's where the shoe pinches."

"I know what you're thinking of," said the willow-tree, sadly. "I can't shade you, since the keeper cut off my nice crown. My long branches up there are all very well and I wouldn't be without them for anything, but they don't give any shade worth talking about and I shall never get another crown, that's quite clear. So you're afraid that the sun will shine too strong on you?"

"Not in the least!" said the dandelion. "The more the sun shines on my yellow face, the better I'm pleased. No, look here, it's the earth I'm anxious about."

"And the most important thing too," said the oak. "But that's the willow-tree's business. If he wants to run an hotel for flowers in his head, he must provide earth: that goes without saying."

"Yes, but is there no earth, my dear Dandelion?" asked the willow-tree.

"There is," said the dandelion. "And good earth too: it's not that. I'm only afraid that there won't be enough of it. You must know, I have a terribly long root: quite a stake, I assure you. When I'm full-grown, there will be at least six inches of it down in the ground."

"Upon my word!" said the oak. "To hear that brat of a dandelion talking about roots!"

The willow-tree stood for a while and said nothing, but thought all the more. The wild rose-bush comforted the dandelion and said nice things about the willow-tree; the elder-bush said it would be all right; the oak grumbled and asked whether, after all, one could expect much from a tree without a crown.

"Now listen," said the willow-tree, who had paid no attention to the others. "I'll tell you something, my dear Dandelion, which I don't generally care to talk about. You know I have had a bad time and have lost my crown?"

"I heard you say so," said the dandelion. "I can also see that you look rather cowed among the other trees in the avenue."

"Don't talk about the poplars," said the willow-tree, distressfully. "They are my relations, but they have never forgiven me for being put here by mistake as a cutting. Look at them and look at me and you can judge for yourself that such a monster as I must be a blot upon a stately avenue of poplars."

"He has some sense of shame left in him," said the nearest poplar.

And all the other trees of the avenue whispered their assent.

"You think about it too much," said the elder-bush. "The more one broods upon a thing, the worse it becomes. I should have died long ago, you know, if I had stood and cried at the losses I have suffered."

"Yes, that's as may be," said the willow-tree. "We all take things in our own way and I in mine. I have not the least intention of throwing up the game, but I know that I am a cripple and shall never be anything else. I thought, a little time ago, that my branches up there would turn into a new crown, but that was sheer folly. They grow and strut and turn green and that is all they do. And then, besides, I feel that I am beginning to decay.

"What's that you say?" asked the wild rose-bush.

"Are you decaying?" asked the oak.

"Yes ... that's by far the worst thing of all," said the elder-bush.

"He's revealing his inmost secrets to the rabble," said the nearest poplar. "Let us stand erect and stiff and whisper and look aloft, dear brothers of the avenue!"

All the poplars whispered.

"I am decaying," said the willow-tree. "I am decaying in my top. How could it be otherwise? There's a puddle up there in summer, the snow lies there in winter and now it's full of moist earth. I can plainly perceive that the hole is growing bigger and bigger, going deeper and deeper inside me. My wood is mouldering away. The shell is good enough still; and I am satisfied as long as it holds out. Then the sap can run up from my roots to my dear, long twigs. Well ... I was thinking the birds will come and visit me, as they are used to, and they will be sure to bring earth with them, so that there will always be more of it as my hole becomes deeper by degrees. And plenty of withered leaves fall on my poor maimed top. I also positively believe that I have an earth-worm up there. How he got there, I don't know: perhaps a bird dropped him out of his beak. But he draws the leaves down into the earth and eats them and turns them into mould. So I say, like the elder-bush, it will be all right."

"So you're becoming hollow?" asked the oak.

"I am," said the willow-tree. "It can't be helped. It's not quite the sort of thing to talk about, but it's different now, because the dandelion was so anxious. It shall never be said of me that I took a respectable flower as a boarder and then let her suffer mortal want."

"Who ever heard a tree talk like that?" said the oak.

"Well, I must say I agree with you this time," said the wild rose-bush.

"I don't think he will hold out very long now," said the elder-bush.

"Thank you, you good old Willow-Tree," said the dandelion. "Now I can go on growing hopefully. I have only this year to think of. When I have sent my seeds into the world with their little parachutes, I shall have done all that is expected of me. I should be delighted if one of them would stay here and grow on you."

"Many thanks," said the willow-tree.

"He accepts the sympathy of the rose-bush and the elder ... he says thank-you to the dandelion ... and he's a relation of ours ... oh, shocking!" said the nearest poplar.

"Shocking ... shocking ... shocking!" whispered the poplars along the avenue.

Then evening came and night; and one and all slept. The wind had gone down, so that there was not even the least whisper in the poplars. But the oak on the little hillock in the fields called out to the willow-tree:

"Pst!... Pst!... Willow-Tree!... Are you asleep?"

"I can't sleep," said the willow-tree. "It's rumbling and gnawing and trickling and seething inside me. I can feel it coming lower and lower. I don't know what it is, but it makes me so melancholy."

"You're becoming hollow," said the oak.

"Perhaps that's what it is," said the willow-tree, sadly. "Well, there's nothing to be done. What can't be cured must be endured."

"Now listen to me, Willow-Tree," said the oak. "On the whole I don't like you."

"I don't know that I ever did you any harm," said the willow-tree.

"Very likely," said the oak. "Only I thought you so arrogant ever since the time when you came the cutting over us. But never mind that now. I have felt most awfully sorry for you since I heard that you were about to become hollow. Take care, that's what I say. It's a terrible misfortune."

"I really don't know what to do to prevent it," said the willow-tree.

"No more do I," said the oak. "But I tell you for all that: take care. See if you can't get all the birds who visit you to scrape all the earth out of the hole in your head before it becomes too deep."

"I mustn't harm the dandelion," said the willow-tree. "Besides, I don't think there's any danger yet. My twigs are green and thriving and my roots are sucking pretty well. As long as the root is sound, everything's sound: you know that as well as I do."

"Take care, that's all," said the oak. "You don't know what it means, but I do. I may as well tell you, I have an old hollow uncle."

"Have you?" said the willow-tree. "Yes, there's a tragedy in every family. You have your uncle and the poplars have me."

"You've no idea of the sort of life he leads," said the oak. "He's awfully old and awfully hollow. Yes, he's like you in a way, but ever so much worse. There's nothing left of him but a very thin shell and just a wretched twig or two in his top. Almost all his roots are dead, too. And he's always full of owls and bats and other vermin. It's a terrible life he leads."

"I'm very sorry to hear it," said the willow-tree.

"I merely say, look out!" said the oak.

And the years came and went and time passed, as it must and will pass.

The willow-tree became more and more decayed and the hole filled with earth and more customers arrived. One spring there was a dainty little sprout, which the tree welcomed under the impression that it was a dandelion.

"Hullo!" said the sprout. "What do you think I am?"

"I have the highest opinion of you," said the willow-tree. "But you are still so small. May I ask your name?"

"I am a strawberry-plant," said the sprout. "And one of the best. My own idea is that I am the equal of those which grow in the manor-garden. Just wait till I get my fruit: then we shall see."

"Goodness me!" said the willow-tree. "If I could only understand where you came from!"

Another sprout came, which proved to be the beginning of a black-currant-bush. A third came, which grew into a dear little mountain-ash. Every summer there were a couple of dandelions. The bees came and buzzed and sucked honey and flew away with it to their hives. The butterflies flitted from flower to flower, sipped a little honey here and there and ate it up. They knew they had to die, so there was no reason for saving it.

"It's wonderful!" said the willow-tree. "If only I knew where all this good fortune comes from!"

"Never mind about that: just take it as it comes," said the elder-bush.

"You will have a fine old age," said the wild rose-bush.

"You're getting hollower and hollower," said the oak. "Remember what I told you about my poor old uncle."

"He has gradually become quite weak-minded," said the nearest poplar.

"Quite weak-minded ... quite weak-minded ... weak-minded," whispered the poplars along the avenue.

The blackbird was the first who had visited the willow-tree and he returned several times each year. One day he came in a great state of fright and asked if he might hide up there. There was a horrid boy who had been shooting at him all the morning with his air-gun:

"I am really preserved at this time of the year," he said. "But what does that brat of a boy care about that? And, if I must lose my life, I would rather be caught in a proper snare."

"I should have thought it would be better to be shot," said the willow-tree. "Then you're done with for good and all."

"I don't agree with you," said the blackbird. "While there's life there's hope. You can always hang on in the snare and struggle and feel that there may be a chance of escaping."

"Yes, indeed," said the willow-tree, pensively. "That's just my case. I also am caught in a trap and know that I must die soon, but I cling to life nevertheless. Well, I have now attained a blessed old age, as the wild rose said. If only I knew where all the dear creatures who grew in my top came from!"

"Well, I can tell you that," said the blackbird. "You may be sure that most of them come from me."

Then he described how fond he was of red berries of every kind. He resorted in particular to the garden of the manor-house, which was full of the nicest things. Then, when he sat and digested his food in the willow-tree, he usually left something behind him, something in the way of one seed or another.

"Is that true?" said the willow-tree. "Yes, of course it's true. So I really owe all my happiness to you!"

"Probably," said the blackbird and whistled with a very consequential air. "We all of us have our mission in this world, thank goodness.... But just look: as I live, there's a beautiful ripe strawberry!"

He ate the strawberry and said, "Hum!" and "Ha!" and "Ho!" for it was so nice:

"It's just as good as those which grow in the squire's own beds," he said. "But I almost think it has got a still nicer flavour by growing up here in you, you old Willow-Tree."

"My dear Blackbird," said the strawberry-plant, "you're often at the manor-house. Won't you do me the favour to tell the squire that I am growing up here?"

"That I will certainly not do," said the blackbird. "In the first place, nothing would induce me to tell any one else where a good berry grows. In the second place, I have been getting so stout and fat lately that I must be a bit careful. Otherwise, it might occur to the squire that strawberries taste twice as nice on top of roast blackbird."

"That's very tiresome," said the strawberry-plant. "I know that the squire has said he will eat no other berries than those which grow in our family; and there are so very few of us. I also heard a bird sing that he had come home from Italy; and I am sure that, if he knew I grew up here, he would himself climb up and pick my berries."

"Lord preserve us!" said the willow-tree. "Would the squire himself really climb into my top? That honour would be greater than I could bear!"

"It certainly would," said the oak. "For you are growing hollower every day. Your long branches are not so green this year as last. You are beginning to look more and more like my unhappy uncle. You're approaching your end, Willow-Tree."

"You may be right," said the willow-tree. "We must all undergo our lot. I myself feel that my shell is getting thinner and thinner; and it has holes in it, besides, in two places down below."

"Away with him!" said the nearest poplar. "He's a disgrace and a reproach to our family."

"Away with him!... Away ... away ... away!" whispered the poplars along the avenue.

9

Time passed and it was incredible that the old willow-tree should still be alive.

His bark had fallen off in great pieces and the holes below had joined in the middle, so that, one day, the fox was able to slip in at one and out at the other. The mice gnawed at the rotten wood. There were only three or four twigs left up above and they were so thin and leafless that it was a pitiful sight to see.

But the garden at the top thrived as it had never done before.

The strawberry-plant put out big flowers which turned into red heavy berries. The black-currant-bush had also grown up and was bearing her fruit. The dandelions shone yellow; and there was also a little blue violet and a scarlet pimpernel, who only opened her flower when the sun shone strongest at noon, and a tall spike of rye, swaying before the wind.

"Why, you're better off now than ever!" said the wild rose-bush. "Since you absolutely had to come to grief and lose your crown, you may well say that fate has been kind to you and made amends to you."

"That's just what I do say," said the willow-tree. "If only I can bear all this good fortune! I am getting thinner and thinner in my shell and every year I lose a twig or two."

"It will end badly," said the oak. "I warned you beforehand. Remember my poor old hollow uncle!"

"I daresay that it will end as it always ends," said the elder-bush. "Whether the end comes one way or another, it is the same for all of us. But I think the willow-tree has life left in him yet."

"There's nothing left to show that he belongs to the family," said the nearest poplar. "His own branches are withering more and more; and it is only strange twigs and leaves that he fans himself with. So that's all right. We sha'n't say a word about his belonging to us: hush!"

"Hush ... hush ... hush!" whispered the poplars along the avenue.

One afternoon the earth-worm crept up there. Hitherto, he had always kept down in the earth, for fear of the many birds about. He was the longest, stoutest, fattest earth-worm in the world.

"Hullo, my dear Earth-Worm, how are you?" said the willow-tree. "I knew you were there, but I have not had the pleasure of seeing you. I am glad you are doing so well in me. How did you come up here exactly?"

"To tell the truth, it was really the blackbird's fault," said the earth-worm. "He dropped me out of his beak. That is to say, he had only got half of me. The rest of me drew back into the ground. So I was only half a worm when I arrived."

"You're welcome all the same," said the willow-tree. "It makes no difference to me if you're whole or half. I myself have lost my crown and become no more than a wretched cripple. But are you all right again now?"

"Oh dear yes!" said the earth-worm. "I don't mind in the least if they chip one end off me. It soon grows again, if only they leave me alone.... But do you know what sort of little sprout this is who is coming up here beside me, with such a funny thick hat on his head?"

"I don't know him," said the willow-tree. "I have become feeble with years and can't at once make out all that grows on me. Do you know him?"

"I should think I ought to!" said the earth-worm. "Why it was I who dragged him into the ground a couple of years ago. He was joined on to a leaf and stalk and I ate up both the leaf and the stalk, but I couldn't manage this chap. That wasn't so odd either, for he was an acorn. Now he has sprouted, he's a little oak."

"An oak!" said the willow-tree, overcome with respectful awe.

"He blew over here in the great storm of the autumn before last," said the earth-worm. "I remember it distinctly, because you were creaking so that I thought it would have been up with all of us."

"What's that you're saying?" said the oak on the little hillock in the fields. "Is one of my children growing on you?"

"Yes," said the old willow-tree. "It's really a little oak. That's a great honour for me."

"It's folly," said the oak. "He must be going to die."

"We all have to die," said the elder-bush.

10

One day the squire came walking down the avenue.

He had the keeper with him and his own two children, a little boy and a little girl. They had not been long at the manor-house and looked about them inquisitively, for everything was new to them.

"What on earth is that ugly old stump doing there?" asked the squire, pointing at the old willow-tree with his cane. "He's enough to spoil the whole avenue. See that you get rid of him to-morrow, keeper. It makes me quite ill to look at him."

For that happened to be his mood that day.

"Now it's coming," said the oak. "That's your death-warrant, you old Willow-Tree. Well, you won't be sorry. I think it must be better to make an end of it than to stand and get hollower day by day."

"We all cling to life," said the willow-tree sadly. "And what will become of my boarders?"

"They may be thankful that they lived so long," said the wild rose-bush.

"Let's first see what happens," said the elder-bush. "I have been through times that looked worse still and have escaped for all that."

"Thank goodness that's over!" said the poplar who stood nearest.

"Thank goodness!... Thank goodness!... Thank goodness!" whispered the poplars along the avenue.

Next morning the keeper came. He had merely an axe with him, for he thought it would only take a couple of blows to do away with the old, rotten willow-stump. Just as he was about to strike, his eyes fell upon the black-currant-bush in the top. The currants were big and ripe. He put out his hand, picked one of them and ate it:

"What a remarkable thing!" he said. "It's exactly like those in the manor-garden. Goodness knows how it got up there!"

'I WANT TO PICK SOME FOR MYSELF'

"Keeper! Keeper!"

The squire's son came running down the avenue. He wanted to see the old willow-tree felled. The keeper told him about the black-currant-bush and picked a currant and gave it to him.

"Lift me up. I must pick some for myself," said the boy.

The keeper lifted him up. He pulled with both hands at the willow-twigs up there and pulled so hard that they snapped.

Then he caught hold of the tree's thin shell, which was so brittle that a big piece came off in each of his hands. But then he clapped his hands with surprise and delight and shouted:

"Keeper! Keeper! There's quite a garden up here. There are the loveliest strawberries beside the black-currant-bush ... and here's a little mountain-ash ... and a dear little oak ... and weeds, too ... five yellow dandelions ... and a spike of barley, keeper.... Oh, how glorious, how glorious! I say, I must show it to sissy ... and to father!"

"Hurry now and eat the strawberries," said the keeper. "For the trunk has to be cut down and then it's all up with the whole concern."

"Lift me down," said the boy, kicking and sprawling. Then, when he stood on the ground, "Don't you dare cut down that tree," he said. "Do you hear? Don't you just dare!"

"Ah, but I do dare!" said the keeper, smiling. "You yourself heard the squire tell me."

"I'm going to run and fetch father," said the boy. "And don't you dare touch the tree before I come back. If you do, trust me, I'll take my revenge on you when I'm squire myself one day!"

Then he ran up the avenue. The keeper sat down in the ditch and waited, for he thought that the wisest thing to do:

"The young rascal has the squire's temper," he said.

"What did I tell you?" said the elder-bush. "You should always listen to those who know."

"It's an awful tension to be in," said the willow-tree. "If only I don't go to pieces for sheer fright. As it is, the boy took a good pull at me; and Heaven knows I can't stand much more!"

"Now you must hold out until we see what happens," said the wild rose-bush. "I have never known anything so exciting."

"Nor I," said the oak. "But it can't end well, when you're hollow to start with."

Then the boy came back with the squire. The little chap pointed and told his story. The keeper rolled a stone up, so that the squire could stand on it and look at the willow-tree's top:

"Well, I never saw anything like it!" he said. "It's quite true: there's a regular garden up there. And my own strawberries, I do believe!"

He picked one and ate it:

"Um!" he said. "Why, that's the genuine flavour! I almost think they're even better than those in the garden."

"And is the tree to be cut down, father?"

"On no account!" said the squire. "It would be a thousand pities. Why, he's the most remarkable tree on the whole estate! See and have a hoop put round him at the top, keeper. And then put a railing round him, so that the cows can't get at him and do him harm. We'll keep this fine old willow-tree as long as we possibly can. I'm exceedingly fond of him."

For that happened to be his mood that day.

An iron hoop was put round the willow-tree's trunk at the top and a railing at the bottom. Every time the squire came driving along the avenue he stopped the carriage at the willow-tree:

"Yes, the avenue is very nice indeed," he said to his guests. "But they're only quite ordinary poplars. Now here I can show you something out of the common. Yes, I know it looks like an old willow-stump, but just come over here...."

They stepped out of the carriage and on to the stone, one after the other, and admired the garden in the willow-tree's top.

"If the hoop wasn't there, I should burst," said the willow-tree. "What an honour and what luck for a wretched cripple like me! Only think: the squire really climbed up and ate strawberries off me! And all the visitors to the manor-house are brought to look at me."

"It's incredible," said the oak. "It's just as though there were a premium on getting hollow."

"It's a romance," said the wild rose-bush. "I'll tell it to every bird that settles on me, so that it may be sung all over the world."

"It's exactly as I told you," said the elder-bush.

"When all is said and done, it was I, in a measure, who prepared the romance," said the blackbird. "But, honestly speaking, I prefer things as they were in the old days. Then one could sit here in peace and quiet. Now we run the risk every moment of somebody or other coming and sticking up his head and saying, 'Well, I never!' or 'Did you ever?' or 'O-oh!' or 'A-ah!'"

"Never in my born days have I known anything like it," said the nearest poplar. "Did you hear how the squire talked of his proud and stately poplars? We, who have stood guard along the road to his manor-house, summer and winter, year after year, all equally straight and still ... quite ordinary poplars, he called us! And then that disgusting, vulgar willow-tree!... That rotten old stump!... And he's a relation of ours into the bargain!... For shame!"

"For shame!... Shame!... Shame!" whispered the poplars along the avenue.

11

One winter's day, a storm came, till all the trees in the wood creaked and crashed. The wind howled and tore down the avenue and all the proud poplars swayed like rushes. The snow drifted till sky and earth became one.

"Now I can hold out no longer," said the old willow-tree.

Then he snapped, right down by his root. The iron hoop which he wore round his head went clattering down the frozen road. The railing tumbled over. The garden up at the top was scattered by the wind in every direction: the black-currant-bush and the strawberry-plant, the mountain-ash and the little oak, the dandelions and the violets all blew away; and nobody knows what has become of them since.

The earth-worm lay just below and wriggled:

"I can't stand this," he said. "Let them chop me into two ... into three.... But this is worse. The ground is as hard as iron: there's not a hole to creep into. And the frost bites my thin skin. Good-bye, all of you: I'm dying!"

In the spring, the stump of the willow-tree was cleared away. But the squire ordered that no new tree should be planted in its stead. Every time he drove past, he told the people with him about the curious old willow-tree that had had quite a garden in his hollow head.

And the wild rose-bush told it to the birds, who sang the story all over the world. The oak could never learn to understand it and the elder-bush said that he had understood it all the time. The blackbird was caught in a snare and eaten.

But the poplars, stately and indignant as ever, still stand and whisper along the avenue.

THE MISTLETOE

1

Just outside the fence of the keeper's garden stood a crab-apple-tree, with crooked branches and apples sour as vinegar.

She had once stood in the middle of a thorn-thicket. But the thorns had died and rotted away; and now the apple-tree stood quite alone in a little green glade.

She was old and ugly and small. She could only just peep over the hazel-hedge into the garden, at the orange-pippin-tree and the russet-apple-tree, who stood and gleamed in the autumn sun with their great red-and-yellow fruit and looked far more important than the crab-apple-tree.

Every morning, the keeper's dog came jogging round the fence to take a mouthful of fresh air and a little exercise. He had lost all his teeth and could see only with one eye. He always stopped for a bit when he came to the crab-apple-tree and rubbed himself against her:

"It's the fleas," said the dog.

"Pray don't mind me in the least," replied the apple-tree. "We have known each other since the days when you were a puppy and the keeper used to thrash you with his whip when you wouldn't obey. I am always delighted to do an old friend a service. By the way, you have plenty of apple-trees nearer at hand ... in there, I mean, in the garden. Why don't you rub yourself against them?"

"Heaven forbid!" the dog. "All honour to the real apple-trees; they are right enough in their way; but you are so beautifully gnarled."

"I am the real apple-tree," said the tree, in an offended tone. "Those in there are only monsters, whom men have deformed for their own use. They grow where the keeper put them and let him pluck them when he pleases; I am wild and free and my own mistress."

The dog rubbed himself and shook his wise old head:

"You ought really to have entered men's service too, old friend," he said. "It's good and snug there. And what else is to become of old fogeys like you and me? Of course, we have to do what is required of us; but then we get what we want in return."

"Perhaps it's there you got your fleas?" asked the apple-tree, sarcastically. "For you certainly have all you want of them!"

But the dog had already jogged back into the garden and did not hear.

Soon after, a blackbird came flying and perched on one of the tree's thickest branches. He flapped his wings and then rubbed his beak against the branch.

"You're welcome," said the apple-tree.

She knew that the blackbird always did like that, after he had been eating, and she was a courteous tree, when no one offended her.

"Thank you," said the blackbird and went on rubbing his beak.

"You're working awfully hard to-day," said the tree.

"There's a stone on the side of my beak," said the blackbird. "It's there as if it were glued fast; and I can't get it off, however much I rub."

"What have you had to eat?"

"I had some beautiful white berries," said the blackbird. "I never tasted anything so good; and I am a judge of berries, as you know. It was somewhere ever so far away; and now I've been flying for a day and a half with this silly stone. Every moment, I've been trying to get it off.... Ah, there it goes, thank goodness! Now it's on you, you old Crab-Apple-Tree. You'll see, you will never get rid of it."

"Just let it be," said the apple-tree, gaily, "and don't bother about me. It'll take to its legs, right enough, when it begins to rain and blow."

The blackbird flew away and the crab-apple-tree stood sunk in her own old thoughts, with the stone on her branch. In the evening, it came on to rain violently and the stone slipped slowly down the wet branch, until it reached the underside.

"Now it will drop," thought the apple-tree.

But the stone did not drop. At night, a terrible storm broke loose and all the trees creaked and swayed to and fro. Inside the keeper's garden, the orange-pippins and the russets fell to the ground by the bushel. But the stone stuck where it was.

"Well, that's odd!" thought the crab-apple-tree.

And, when the dog came jogging along in the morning, the tree told him of the queer thing:

"What sort of a chap can it be?" she asked.

"I expect it's a flea," said the dog and rubbed himself. "One can never get rid of them. Does it hop all over you? And bite you?"

"Certainly not," replied the apple-tree. "Last night, it slipped down quite gently to the underside of the branch; and, for that matter, it does me no harm."

"Then it's not a flea," said the dog.

Autumn came and all the good apples in the garden were gathered and stored in the loft. There was no one who cared about the crab-apple-tree. Her apples remained on the branches till they fell to the ground, where they lay and rotted. But the tree was well-pleased with the state of things. She knew that little crab-apple-trees would sprout from them and that was why she had put them forth.

Then winter came, with frost and snow. The old dog lay all day under the stove in the parlour. The crab-apple-tree stood outside in the snow, with the queer stone under her branch.

When spring returned, the dog, one day, came jogging round the fence.

THE OLD DOG STOOD ON HIS HIND-LEGS AND BLINKED WITH HIS BLIND EYES

It took longer than last year and he was now almost quite blind in the other eye as well. But he found his way to the apple-tree and rubbed himself, so that she saw that he still had those fleas.

"All going as usual, Dog?"

"Yes, Apple-Tree.... Same with you?"

"Well, I'll tell you," said the tree. "I daresay you remember that stone the blackbird brought me? Well, look here, some time ago, I felt a most curious pricking and itching and aching just where it was."

"Then it *must* be a flea," said the dog.

"Now listen," said the tree. "It was a most unpleasant sensation. And then my branch swelled up at the place where the stone was...."

"It's a flea, it's a flea!" cried the dog. "There's no doubt about it. Just rub yourself up against me, old Apple-Tree! It's only fair that I should make you a return for your kindness."

"What does a flea look like?" asked the apple-tree.

"We-ell," said the dog and rubbed himself. "They're that sort of chaps, you know, that one really never has time to see them."

"Has a flea green leaves?"

"Not that I know of," said the dog.

"Come and look up here," said the tree. "There ... on my lowest branch ... just above your head ... is that a flea?"

The old dog stood on his hind-legs and blinked with his blind eyes:

"I can't see so far," he said. "But I have never been able to see the fleas on my own tail, so that doesn't mean anything."

Then he slunk away.

But, a little later, a thin voice came from the apple-tree's branch and said:

"I am not a flea. I am the mistletoe."

"Well, I'm no wiser," said the apple-tree.

"I'm a plant like yourself," said the voice. "I shall turn into a bush ... with roots and branches and flowers and leaves and all the rest of it."

"Then why don't you grow in the ground like us?" asked the crab-apple-tree.

"That happens not to be my nature," said the mistletoe.

"Then you have a nasty nature," said the apple-tree and shook herself furiously, so that her white blossoms trembled. "For I understand this much, that I shall have to feed you, you sluggard!"

"Yes, please, if you will be so good," said the mistletoe. "I have my roots fixed in you already; and I am growing day by day. Later on, I shall put forth little green blossoms. They're not much to look at; but then the berries will come, beautiful, juicy white berries: the blackbird is quite mad on them."

"The blackbird is a very fine bird," said the apple-tree; "but, if he wants to dine off me, he can eat my own apples."

"You mustn't think that I have berries for the blackbird's sake," said the mistletoe. "Inside the berry there is a stone; and in the stone my seed lies. And the stone is so sticky that it hangs tight on to the blackbird's beak, until he manages to rub it off on some good old apple-tree or other, who will be a foster-mother to my children, as you have been to me."

"You're a nice family, upon my word!" said the apple-tree. "Aren't you ashamed to live upon other people's labour? And can't you cast your seed on the ground, as every one else does, and leave it to look after itself?"

"No," said the mistletoe, "I can't. But it's no use my explaining that to you. There is something mysterious and refined about me that raises me above the common trees. Men and women understand it. They have surrounded me with beautiful and curious legends and ballads. Just think, over in England they simply can't keep Christmas without hanging a bunch of me from the ceiling. Then, when they dance and come under the bunch, they are allowed to kiss each other."

"Pooh!" said the crab-apple-tree. "That's nothing to talk about. Why, there isn't an engaged couple in the whole parish but has sat in my shade and kissed."

"You miss the point of it, old friend," said the mistletoe. "Engaged couples can kiss wherever they please. But those who dance under the mistletoe may kiss each other even if they are not engaged."

"You horrid, immoral foreigner!" said the apple-tree. "But one can't expect anything else from the sort of life you lead. Well, it's to be hoped that you'll freeze to bits in the winter."

"Indeed, I shall do no such thing," replied the mistletoe. "When your leaves are withered and fallen and you stand strutting with your bare branches in the snow, mine will be just as fresh and green as now. I am *evergreen* you must know: green in winter and green in spring."

The crab-apple-tree was so exasperated that she was quite unable to reply. But, when the dog came next day, she told him all about it.

"Then he is a flea, after all," said the old dog. "In a fashion. You must manage to rub him off you: that's the only thing that helps a bit."

"I am not a dog to run and rub myself," said the apple-tree. "But, all the same, it's hard for a respectable tree to have to put up with this sort of thing in her old age."

"Take it calmly now!" said the mistletoe. "Who knows but that you'll end by being glad to have me?"

The next summer, an old professor, with a pair of spectacles on his nose and a great botanizing-case on his back, came roaming through the wood.

He sat down under the crab-apple-tree to eat his lunch, but fell a-thinking in the middle of it, leant his head back against the trunk and looked up into the leaves.

Suddenly he jumped up, dropped his sandwich and stared hard at the mistletoe. He took off his spectacles, wiped them on the skirt of his coat, put them back on his nose and went on staring.

Then he ran in and fetched the old keeper:

"Keeper, do you see that tree?" he said. "That's the most remarkable tree in the whole wood."

"That one there?" said the keeper. "Why, it's only an old crab-apple-tree, professor. You should see a couple of apple-trees I have in my garden."

"I don't care a fig for them," said the professor. "I would give all the apple-trees in the world for this one tree. There's a mistletoe growing on her, you must know, and the mistletoe is the rarest plant in Denmark. You must put a fence round the tree at once, so that no one can hurt her. For, if she dies, then the mistletoe dies too."

And a fence was put round the old apple-tree. The professor wrote about her in the newspapers; and every one who came to the neighbourhood had to go and look at the mistletoe.

"Well?" said the mistletoe.

"My dear little foster-child," said the crab-apple-tree, "if there's anything you require, do, for goodness' sake, say so!"

When the keeper's old dog came out and wanted to rub himself, he remained standing in amazement and looked at the fence with his one, half-blind eye.

"You can go back to the garden and rub yourself against the *real* apple-trees!" said the crab-apple-tree, haughtily. "I stand here with a mistletoe and must be treated with the utmost care. If I die, the mistletoe dies: do you understand? I have been written about in the papers. I am the most important tree in the wood!"

"Yes ... you're all that!" said the dog and jogged home again.

THE LILAC-BUSH

1

There was a terrible commotion in the lilac-bush.

Not a breath of wind was blowing; and yet the branches shook from top to bottom and all the leaves quivered so that it hurt one's eyes to see.

The chaffinch perched upon the bush for his after-dinner nap, as was his wont; but the branches shook under him to such an extent that he could not close an eye and he flew away quite frightened to the laburnum. He asked his wife what on earth could be the matter with that decent bush; but she was sitting on her eggs and was too busy to answer. Then he asked his neighbour, the tit; and the tit scratched his black skull-cap and shook his head mysteriously:

"I don't understand bush-language," he said. "But there's something wrong. I noticed it myself this morning, when I was sitting over there, singing."

Then he sat down in the laburnum beside the chaffinch and both of them stared at the queer bush.

Now the only thing the matter with the lilac-bush was that the root had turned sulky:

"Here I have to sit and drudge for the whole family!" he growled. "It is I who do all the work. I must provide food for the branches and the leaves and the flowers and hold them fast besides, else the wind would soon blow the whole lot away. And who gives a thought to a faithful servant like me? Does it ever occur to those fine fellows up there that somebody else might also need a little recreation? I hear them talk of the spring and sunshine and all that sort of thing; but I myself never get a bit of it. I don't even know for certain what it means; I only know that in the spring they all eat like mad. It's quite a decent place in the winter: then there's no more to do than a fellow can manage; and it's snug and cosy in here. But a root has a regular dog's life of it as soon as the air turns warm."

"Catch good hold of the earth, you old root!" cried the branches. "The wind's rising, there's a storm brewing!"

"Send us up some more food, you black root!" whispered the leaves. "It will be long before the whole family has done growing."

Then the flowers began to sing:

>"Water's a boon;
>Send us some soon!
>For, in fierce heat,
>Drinking is sweet.
>Then grant our suit,
>You ugly root;
>Send water, pray,
>This way!"

"Ah, isn't that just what I said?" growled the root. "It's I who bear all the brunt. But we'll soon put an end to that. I want to come up and have a good wash in the rain and let the sun shine on me, so that people can see that I am quite as good as the rest. Hullo, you dandy branches, who are not twopence-worth of use! I'm sick and tired of working for a pack of idlers like you. I'm coming up to take a holiday. Hold tight, for I'm letting go!"

"Idlers, indeed!" cried the branches. "That's all you know about it, you silly root! We certainly do at least as much as you."

"You?" asked the root. "What do you do, I should like to know?"

"We straddle all day long to lift up the green leaves in the sunshine," replied the branches. "We have to spread ourselves on every side, so that they may all get the same amount. If you could look up here, you would see that some of us are crooked with the mere effort. No, you can call the leaves idlers, if you must needs have somebody to vent your sulks upon."

The root pondered upon this for a while and at last came to the conclusion that it was very sensible. And then he began storming frightfully at the green leaves:

"How long do you think that I mean to be your servant?" he growled. "I give you notice, from the first of the month, I do! Then you can turn to and do some work for yourselves, you lazy leaves!"

The branches now began to scold in their turn and cried to the leaves:

"The root is right! You must make yourselves useful, that's what we say too. We are tired of carrying you."

And they creaked loudly to emphasize their remarks.

"Fair and softly, you black root!" whispered the leaves. "And, if you were not so consequential, you long branches, you would not shout loud, for, after all, it's annoying to have people find out what dunces you are. Do you imagine that we have not our task as well as you?"

"Let's hear, let's hear!" said the branches, drawing themselves up.

"Let's hear about it!" said the root, making himself as stiff as he could.

"Now don't you know that it's we who prepare the food?" whispered the leaves. "Do you imagine that decent folk can eat it raw, just as the root takes it out of the ground and sends it up through the branches? No, it has to come up to us first; and, when we receive it, we light a fire and cook away in the sun's rays until it's all ready and fit to eat. Do you call that being no use?"

"We-ell!" said the branches, creaking in an embarrassed sort of fashion. "There may be something in that."

They began to explain it to the root, who had not quite understood, and he also thought that it sounded very reasonable.

A little later, the leaves began to whisper again:

"Since you absolutely must have some one to abuse, why not go for the flowers? They are more smartly dressed than any of us; they live at the top of the tree, nearest to the sun. And what do they do? Perhaps you know, for, upon my word, we don't!"

"Quite right!" growled the root. "We won't submit to it any longer. Please render an account of yourselves, you lazy, dressed-up flowers! What are you good for? Why should we others drudge and toil for you?"

The flowers rocked softly to and fro and wafted their fragrance in the air. The others had to ask three times before they got an answer; but then the flowers sang:

"Where sunlight is streaming,
We float, ever dreaming..."

"Yes, we believe you!" said the leaves. "And do you call that working?"

But the flowers sang again:

>"Where sunlight is streaming,
>We float, ever dreaming
>Of light and happiness and love,
>Of all the glory of heaven above,
>Of buds which at last through black earth shall rise
>With thousands of tiny, lilac eyes."

"Bosh!" whispered the leaves and "Bosh!" cried the branches and "Bosh!" growled the root, on receiving this explanation.

They all agreed that it was a great shame that they should work for those lazy flowers. And they shook and creaked and whispered and cried and growled for sheer rage; and it became a terrible commotion.

But the flowers only laughed at them and sang:

> "Grumble, root, and whisper, leaf!
> No flower feels the slightest grief.
> Long brown shoots, for all your screaming,
> Not a flower is baulked of dreaming!"

3

The summer passed and it was autumn.

The young green branches put on their winter coats. The leaves had no winter coats. They took great offence at this and were not content until they had vexed themselves into a jaundice. Then they died. One by one, they fell to the ground and at last they lay in a great heap over the old, cross-grained root.

But the flowers had long since gone to the wall. In their stead were a number of queer, ugly things that rustled whenever the wind blew. And, when the first storm of winter had passed over the lilac-bush, they also fell off and there was nothing left but the bare branches.

"Oh dear!" sighed the branches. "We wouldn't mind changing with you now, you black root. You're having a nice cosy time in the ground just now."

The root did not reply, for he had got something to meditate on. Close beside him, you must know, lay a singular little thing which he simply couldn't make out at all.

"What sort of a fellow are you?" asked the root, but received no answer.

"Can't you answer when you're spoken to by respectable people?" said the root again. "Seeing that we're neighbours, it seems reasonable that we should make each other's acquaintance."

But the queer thing persisted in saying nothing and the root meditated all through the winter and wondered what it could be.

Later, in the spring, the thing swelled out and grew ever so fat and, one day, a little sprout shot out of it.

"Good-morning!" said the root. "A merry spring-time to you! Perhaps you will now think fit to answer what I have been asking you these last six months: whom have I the honour of addressing?"

"I am the flowers' dream," replied the thing. "I am a seed and you are a blockhead."

The root pondered about this for some little time. He did not mind being called a blockhead, for, when you're a root, you have to submit to being abused. But he couldn't quite understand that remark about the flowers' dream and so he begged for a further explanation.

"I can feel that the ground is still too hard for me to break through," said the seed, "so I don't mind having a chat with you. You see, I was lying inside one of the flowers, when you others were squabbling with them in the summer, and I heard all that you said. I had a fine laugh at you, believe me; but I dared not join in the conversation: I was too green for that."

"Well, but, now that you are big, I suppose you're allowed to talk?" asked the root.

"Big enough not to care a fig for you!" replied the seed and, at the same time, shot a dear little root into the ground. "I have a root of my own now and need not submit to any of your impudence."

The old root opened his eyes very wide indeed, but said nothing.

"However, I prefer to treat you with civility," said the seed. "After all, in a manner of speaking, you're my father."

"Am I?" asked the root and looked as important as ever he could.

"Of course you are," replied the seed. "You are all of you my parents. You procured food for me in the earth and the leaves cooked it in the sun. The branches lifted me into the air and light, but the flower rocked me in the bottom of her calyx and dreamed and, in her dream, whispered in the ears of the bumblebees, so that they might tell it to the other lilacs. You all gave me of your best; I owe my whole life to you."

This gave the root something to think about. It was almost midsummer before he solved the problem. But, when he had got it thoroughly into his stupid head, he asked the branches, in an unusually civil voice, whether there was not a fine little lilac-bush standing near them.

"Certainly there is!" replied the branches. "But you just attend to your business! It's blowing hard enough to topple us all over this very moment."

"Never you fear!" said the root. "I shall hold tight enough. I only wanted to tell you that that little lilac-bush is my child."

"Ha, ha, ha!" laughed the branches. "Do you think an old black root like you can get such a sweet little child as that? It's prettier and fresher and greener than you can imagine."

"It's my child for all that," said the root, proudly.

And then he told the branches what he had heard from the seed; and the branches repeated it to all the leaves.

"Well, there!" they all said; and then they understood that they were a big family, in which each had his own work to see to.

"Hush!" they said to one another. "Let us be careful not to disturb the flowers in their dream."

And the old root toiled away, as if he were paid for it, to provide lots of food; and the branches stretched and pushed and twisted awfully to supply proper light and air; and the leaves fluttered in the warm summer breeze and looked as if they were doing nothing at all; but, inside them, there was roasting and stewing in thousands of little kitchens.

And up at the top of the bush sat the flowers and dreamed and sang:

> "Dear little seed, sing lullaby!
> Leaves shall fall and flowers shall die.
> You, in the black earth singing low,
> Into a bonny bush shall grow,
> A bush with leaves and flowers
> Scenting June's glad hours!"

THE BEECH AND THE OAK

1

It was in the old days.

There were no towns with houses and streets and towering church-steeples. There were no schools. For there were not many boys; and those there were learnt from their fathers to shoot with a bow and arrow, to hunt the deer in his hiding-place, to kill the bear in order to make clothes of his skin and to get fire by rubbing two pieces of wood together. When they knew all this thoroughly, their education was completed.

Nor were there any railways, or tilled fields, or ships on the sea, or books, for there was nobody who could read them.

There was hardly anything but trees.

But then of trees there were plenty. They stood everywhere from coast to coast, mirrored themselves in every river and lake and stretched their mighty branches up into the sky. They stooped over the sea-shore, dipped their branches in the black water of themarshes and looked haughtily over the land from the tall hills.

They all knew one another, for they belonged to one big family and they were proud of it:

"We are all oak-trees," they said and drew themselves up. "We own the land and we govern it."

And they were quite right, for there were only very few people at that time. Otherwise there was nothing but wild animals. The bear, the wolf and the fox went hunting, while the deer grazed by the edge of the marsh.

The wood-mouse sat outside her hole and ate acorns and the beaver built his ingenious house on the river-bank.

Then, one day, the bear came trudging along and lay down at full length under a great oak-tree.

"Are you there again, you robber?" said the oak and shook a heap of withered leaves over him.

'YOU REALLY OUGHT NOT TO BE SO WASTEFUL WITH YOUR LEAVES, OLD FRIEND,' SAID THE BEAR, LICKING HIS PAWS.

"You really ought not to be so wasteful with your leaves, old friend," said the bear, licking his paws. "They are the only thing you have to keep off the sun with."

"If you don't like me, you can go," replied the oak, proudly. "I am lord of the land and, look where you may, you will find none but my brothers."

"True enough," growled the bear. "That's just the tiresome part of it. I've been for a little trip abroad, you see, and have been a bit spoilt. That was in a country down south. I took a nap under the beech-trees there. They are tall, slender trees, not crooked old fellows like you. And their tops are so dense that the sunbeams can't pierce through them at all. It was a real delight to sleep there of an afternoon, believe me."

"Beech-trees?" asked the oak, curiously. "What are they?"

"You might wish that you were half so handsome as a beech-tree," said the bear. "But I'm not going to gossip with you any more just now. I've had to trot over a mile in front of a confounded hunter, who caught me on one of my hind-legs with an arrow. Now I want to sleep; and perhaps you will be so kind as to provide me with rest, since you can't provide me with shade."

The bear lay down and closed his eyes, but there was no sleep for him this time. For the other trees had heard what he said and there came such a chattering and a jabbering and a rustling of leaves as had never been known in the forest:

"Heaven knows what sort of trees those are!" said one.

"Of course, it's a story which the bear wants us to swallow," said another.

"What can trees be like whose leaves are so close together that the sunbeams can't pierce them through?" asked a little oak who had been listening to what the big ones were saying.

But next to him stood an old, gnarled tree, who slapped the little oak on the head with one of his lower branches:

"Hold your tongue," he said, "and don't talk till you have something to say. And you others need not believe a word of the bear's nonsense. I am much taller than you and I can see a long way over the forest. But as far away as I can see there is nothing but oak-trees."

The little oak remained shamefaced and silent and the other big trees whispered softly to one another, for they had a great respect for the old one.

But the bear got up and rubbed his eyes:

"Now you have disturbed my afternoon nap," he growled, angrily, "and I shall have my revenge on you, never fear. When I come back, I shall bring some beech-seed with me and I'll answer for it that you will all turn yellow with envy when you see how handsome the new trees are."

Then he trotted away.

But the oaks talked to one another for days at a time of the queer trees which he had told them of:

"If they come, we'll do for them!" said the little oak-tree.

But the old oak gave him one on the head:

"If they come," he said, "you'll be civil to them, you puppy. But they won't come."

But this was where the old oak was wrong, for they did come.

In the autumn, the bear returned and lay down under the old oak:

"I am to give you the kind regards of the people down below there," he said and picked some funny things off his shaggy coat. "Just look what I've got for you."

"What's that?" asked the oak.

"That's beech," replied the bear. "Beech-seed, as I promised you."

Then he trampled the seed into the earth and prepared to leave again:

"It's a pity I can't stay to see how annoyed you will be," he said, "but those dashed human beings have become so troublesome. They killed my wife and one of my brothers the other day and I must look out for a place where I can dwell in peace. There is hardly a spot left for an honest bear to live in. Good-bye, you gnarled old oak-trees!"

When the bear had jogged off, the trees looked at one another seriously:

"Let's see what happens," said the old oak.

And, when the spring came, the grass was green and the birds began to sing where they last left off. The flowers swarmed up from the ground and everything looked fresh and vigorous.

The oaks alone still stood with leafless branches:

"It is very distinguished to come last," they said to one another. "The king of the forest does not arrive before the whole company is assembled."

But at last they did arrive. All the leaves burst forth from the fat buds and the trees looked at one another and complimented one another on their good appearance. The little oak had grown a decent bit. This made him feel important and think that he now had a right to join in the conversation:

"There's not much coming of the bear's beech-trees," he said, mockingly, but at the same time glanced up anxiously at the old oak who used to slap his head.

The old oak heard what he said and so did the others. But they said nothing. None of them had forgotten what the bear had said and, every morning, when the sun shone, they peeped down stealthily to see if the beeches had come. At bottom, they were a little uneasy, but they were too proud to talk about it.

And, one day, at last, the little sprouts shot up from the ground. The sun shone upon them and the rain fell over them, so that it was not long before they grew to a good height.

"I say, how pretty they are!" said the great oaks and twisted their crooked branches still more, so as to see them better.

"You are welcome among us," said the old oak and gave them a gracious nod. "You shall be my foster-children and have just as good a time as my own."

"Thank you," said the little beeches and not a word more.

But the little oak did not like the strange trees:

"It's awful, the way you're shooting up," he said, in a vexed tone. "You're already half as tall as I am. May I beg you to remember that I am much older than you and of a good family besides?"

The beeches laughed with their tiny little green leaves, but said nothing.

"Shall I bend my branches a little to one side, so that the sun may shine on you better?" asked the old tree, politely.

"Much obliged," replied the beeches, "but we can grow quite nicely in the shade."

And all the summer passed and another summer and still more. The beeches kept on growing steadily and at last grew right over the little oak's head.

"Keep your leaves to yourselves," cried the oak. "You're standing in my light; and that I can't endure. I must have proper sunshine. Take your leaves away, or else I shall die."

The beeches only laughed and went on growing. At last they met right over the little oak's head and then he died.

"That was ill done," roared the big oaks and shook their branches in anger.

But the old oak stood up for his foster-children:

"Serve him right!" he said. "That's his reward for bragging. I say it, though he is my own flesh and blood. But you must be careful now, you little beeches, or else I shall slap you on the head too."

The years passed and the beeches kept on growing and gradually became slim young trees that reached right up among the old oak's branches.

"You're beginning to be rather intrusive for my taste," said the old oak. "You should try to grow a bit thicker and stop this shooting into the air. Just look how your branches stick out. Bend them decently, as you see us do. How will you manage when a regular storm comes? Take it from me, the wind shakes the tree-tops finely! He has many a time come whistling through my old branches; and how do you think that you'll come off, with that flimsy finery which you stick up in the air?"

"Every one grows in his own manner and we in ours," replied the young beeches. "This is the way it's done where we come from; and we daresay we are quite as good as you."

"That's not a polite remark to make to an old tree with moss on his branches," said the oak. "I am beginning to regret that I was so kind to you. If you have a scrap of honour in your composition, just have the goodness to move your leaves a little to one side. Last year, there were hardly any buds on my lower branches, all through your standing in my light."

"We can't quite see what that has to do with us," replied the beeches. "Every one has enough to do to look after himself. If he is industrious and successful, then things go well with him. If not, he must be content to go to the wall. Such is the way of the world."

And the oak's lower branches died and he began to be terribly frightened:

"You're nice fellows, you are!" he said. "The way you reward me for my hospitality! When you were little, I let you grow at my foot and sheltered you against the storm. I let the sun shine on you whenever he wanted to and I treated you as if you were my own children. And now you choke me, by way of thanks."

"Fudge!" said the beeches. Then they blossomed and put forth fruit; and, when the fruit was ripe, the wind shook their branches and scattered it all around.

"You are active people like myself," said the wind. "That's why I like you and will gladly give you a hand."

And the fox rolled at the foot of the beech and filled his coat with the prickly fruit and ran all over the country with it. The bear did the same and moreover laughed at the old oak while he lay and rested in the shadow of the beech. The wood-mouse was delighted with the new food which she got and thought that beech-nuts tasted much better than acorns.

New little beeches shot up around and grew just as quickly as their parents and looked as green and happy as if they did not know what a bad conscience was.

And the old oak gazed out sadly over the forest. The bright-green beech-leaves peeped forth on every hand and the oaks sighed and told one another their troubles:

"They are taking our power from us," they said and shook themselves as well as they could for the beeches. "The land is no longer ours."

One branch died after the other and the storm broke them off and flung them to the ground. The old oak had now only a few leaves left in his top:

"The end is at hand," he said, gravely.

But there were many more people in the land now than there had been before and they hastened to cut down the oaks while there were still some left:

"Oak makes better timber than beech," they said.

"So at last we get a little appreciation," said the old oak. "But we shall have to pay for it with our lives."

Then he said to the beech-trees:

"What was I thinking of, when I helped you on in your youth? What an old fool I have been! We oak-trees used to be lords in the land; and now, year after year, I have had to see my brothers all around perish in the struggle against you. I myself am almost done for; and not one of my acorns has sprouted, thanks to your shade. But, before I die, I should like to know what you call your behaviour."

"That's soon said, old friend!" answered the beeches. "We call it *competition*; and it's no discovery of ours. It's what rules the world."

"I don't know those outlandish words of yours," said the oak. "*I* call it base ingratitude."

Then he died.

'HIDE ME! SAVE ME!'

THE WEEDS

1

It was a fine and fruitful year.

Rain and sunshine came turn and turn about, in just the way that was best for the corn. As soon as the farmer thought that things were getting rather dry, he could be quite sure that it would rain next day. And, if he considered that he had had rain enough, then the clouds parted at once, just as though it were the farmer that was in command.

The farmer, therefore, was in a good humour and did not complain as he usually did. Cheerful and rejoicing he walked over the land with his two boys:

"It will be a splendid harvest this year," he said. "I shall get my barns full and make lots of money. Then Jens and Ole shall have a new pair of trousers apiece and I will take them with me to market."

"If you don't cut me soon, farmer, I shall be lying down flat," said the rye and bowed her heavy ears right down to the ground.

Now the farmer could not hear this, but was quite able to see what the rye was thinking of; and so he went home to fetch his sickle.

"It's a good thing to be in the service of men," said the rye. "I can be sure now that all my grains will be well taken care of. Most of them will go to the mill and that, certainly, is not very pleasant. But afterwards they will turn into beautiful new bread; and one must suffer something for honour's sake. What remains the farmer will keep and sow next year on his land."

Along the hedge and beside the ditch stood the weeds. Thistle and burdock, poppy and bell-flower and dandelion grew in thick clusters and all had their heads full of seed. For them, too, it had been a fruitful year, for the sun shines and the rain falls on the poor weeds just as much as on the rich corn.

"There's no one to cut us and cart us to the barn," said the dandelion and shook her head, but very carefully, lest the seed should fall too soon. "What is to become of our children?"

"It gives me a headache to think of it," said the poppy. "Here I stand, with many hundreds of seeds in my head, and I have no idea where to dispose of them."

"Let's ask the rye's advice," said the burdock.

And then they asked the rye what they ought to do.

"It doesn't do to mix in other people's affairs when one's well off," said the rye. "There is only one piece of advice that I will give you: mind you don't fling your silly seed over my field, or you'll have me to deal with!"

Now this advice was of no use to the wild flowers; and they stood all day pondering as to what they should do. When the sun went down, they closed their petals to go to sleep, but they dreamt all night of their seed and next morning they had found a remedy.

The poppy was the first to wake.

She carefully opened some little shutters in the top of her head, so that the sun could shine right in upon the seeds. Next, she called to the morning wind, who was running and playing along the hedge:

"Dear Wind," she said, pleasantly. "Will you do me a service?"

"Why not?" said the wind. "I don't mind having something to do."

"It's a mere trifle," said the poppy. "I will only ask you to give a good shake to my stalk, so that my seeds can fly away out of the shutters."

"Right you are," said the wind.

And away flew the seeds to every side. The stalk certainly snapped; but that the poppy did not bother about. For, when one has provided for one's children, there's really nothing left to do in this world.

"Good-bye," said the wind and wanted to go on.

"Wait a bit," said the poppy. "Promise me first that you won't tell the others. Else they might have the same ideas; and then there would be less room for my seeds."

"I shall be silent as the grave," said the wind and ran away.

"Pst! Pst!" said the bell-flower. "Have you a moment to do me a tiny service?"

"All right," said the wind. "What is it?"

"Oh, I only wanted to ask you to shake me a little!" said the flower. "I have opened some shutters in my head and I should like to have my seeds sent a good distance out into the world. But you must be sure not to tell the others, or they might think of doing the same thing."

"Lord preserve us!" said the wind and laughed. "I shall be dumb as a fish."

And then he gave the flower a thorough good shaking and went on.

"Dear Wind, dear Wind!" cried the dandelion. "Where are you off to so fast?"

"Is there anything the matter with you too?" asked the wind.

"Not a bit," said the dandelion. "I only wanted to have a word with you."

"Then be quick about it," said the wind, "for I am thinking seriously of going down."

"You see," said the dandelion, "it's very difficult for us this year to get all our seed settled; and yet one would like to do the best one can for one's children. How the bell-flower and the poppy and the poor burdock will manage I do not know, upon my word. But the thistle and I have put our heads together and have hit upon an expedient. You must help us."

"That makes four in all," thought the wind and could not help laughing aloud.

"What are you laughing at?" asked the dandelion. "I saw you whispering with the bell-flower and the poppy just now; but, if you give them the least hint, I won't tell you a thing."

"What do you take me for?" said the wind. "Mum's the word! What is it you want?"

"We've put a nice little umbrella up at the top of our seed. It's the sweetest little toy that you can think of. If you only just blow on me, it will fly up in the air and fall down wherever you please. Will you?"

"Certainly," said the wind.

And—whoosh!—he blew over the thistle and the dandelion and carried all their seed with him across the fields.

The burdock still stood pondering. She was thick-headed and that was why she took so long. But, in the evening, a hare jumped over the hedge:

"Hide me! Save me!" he cried. "Farmer's Trust is after me."

"Creep round behind the hedge," said the burdock; "then I'll hide you."

"You don't look to me as if you were cut out for that job," said the hare; "but beggars can't be choosers."

And then he hid behind the hedge.

"Now, in return, you might take some of my seeds to the fields with you," said the burdock; and she broke off some of her many burs and scattered them over the hare.

Soon after, Trust came running along the hedge.

"Here's the dog!" whispered the burdock; and, with a bound, the hare leapt over the hedge into the rye.

"Have you seen the hare?" asked Trust. "I can see that I'm too old for hunting. One of my eyes is quite blind and my nose can no longer find the scent."

"I have seen him," replied the burdock, "and, if you will do me a service, I will show you where he is."

Trust agreed and the burdock struck some of her burs in his back and said:

"Would you just rub yourself against the stile here, inside the field? But that's not where you're to look for the hare, for I saw him run to the wood a little while ago."

Trust carried the burs to the field and ran off into the wood.

"So now I've got my seeds settled," said the burdock and laughed to herself contentedly. "But goodness knows how the thistle is going to manage and the dandelion and the bell-flower and the poppy!"

Next spring, already, the rye was standing quite high:

"We are very well off, considering all things," said the rye-stalks. "Here we are in a great company that contains none but our own good family. And we don't hamper one another in the very least. It's really an excellent thing to be in the service of men."

But, one fine day, a number of little poppies and thistles and dandelions and burdocks and bell-flowers stuck their heads up above the ground in the midst of the luxuriant rye.

"What's the meaning of this now?" asked the rye. "How in the world did you get here?"

And the poppy looked at the bell-flower and asked:

"How did you get here?"

And the thistle looked at the burdock and asked:

"How on earth did you get here?"

They were all equally surprised and it was some time before they had done explaining. But the rye was the angriest and, when she had heard all about Trust and the hare and the wind, she was quite furious:

"Thank goodness that the farmer shot the hare in the autumn," said she. "Trust, luckily, is dead too, the old scamp! So I have no further quarrel with *them*. But how dare the wind carry the seed of the weeds on to the farmer's land!"

"Softly, softly, you green Rye!" said the wind, who had been lying behind the hedge and had heard all this. "I ask no one's leave, but do as I please; and now I'm going to make you bow before me."

Then he blew over the young rye so that the thin stalks swayed to and fro:

"You see," he said, "the farmer looks after his rye, for that is his business. But the rain and the sun and I interest ourselves in all of you alike, without distinction of persons. To us the poor weeds are quite as attractive as the rich corn."

Now the farmer came out to look at his rye and, when he saw the weeds that stood in the fields, he was vexed and scratched his head and began to scold in his turn:

"That's that dirty Wind," he said to Jens and Ole, who stood beside him with their hands in the pockets of their new trousers.

But the wind dashed up and blew off the hats of all three of them and trundled them ever so far away. The farmer and his boys ran after them, but the wind was the quicker. At last, he rolled the hats into the pond; and the farmer and his boys had to stand ever so long and fish for them before they got them out.

The ANEMONES

1

"Peewit! Peewit!" cried the lapwing, as he flew over the bog in the wood. "Dame Spring is coming! I can feel it in my legs and wings."

When the new grass, which lay below in the earth, heard this, it at once began to sprout and peeped out gaily from between the old yellow straw. For the grass is always in an immense hurry.

Now the anemones in among the trees had also heard the lapwing's cry, but refused on any account to appear above the earth:

"You mustn't believe the lapwing," they whispered to one another. "He's a flighty customer and not to be trusted. He always comes too early and starts calling at once. No, we will wait quietly till the starling and the swallow come. They are sensible, sober people, who are not to be taken in and who know what they are about."

And the starlings came.

They perched on a twig outside their summer villa and looked about them:

"Too early, as usual," said Mr. Starling. "Not a green leaf and not a fly, except an old tough one of last year, not worth opening one's beak for."

Mrs. Starling said nothing, but looked none too cheerful either.

"If we had only remained in our snug winter-quarters beyond the mountains!" said Mr. Starling. He was angry because his wife did not answer, for he was so cold that he thought a little discussion might do him good. "But it's *your* fault, just as last year. You're always in such a terrible hurry to come out to the country."

"If I'm in a hurry, I know the reason why," said Mrs. Starling. "And it would be a shame for you if you didn't know too, for they are your eggs just as much as mine."

"Heaven forbid!" replied Mr. Starling, indignantly. "When have I denied my family? Perhaps you expect me, over and above, to sing to you in the cold?"

"Yes, that I do!" said Mrs. Starling, in the tone which he could not resist.

He at once began to whistle as best he could. But, when Mrs. Starling had heard the first notes, she flapped her wings and pecked at him with her beak:

"Will you be quiet at once!" she screamed, angrily. "It sounds so dismal that it makes one feel quite melancholy. You'd better see to it that the anemones come up. I think it's high time. And, besides, one always feels warmer when there are others shivering too."

Now, as soon as the anemones had heard the starling's first whistle, they carefully stuck their heads out of the ground. But they were still so tightly tucked up in their green wraps that one could hardly see them. They looked like green buds that might turn into anything.

"It's too early," they whispered. "It's a shame for the starling to call us. There's no one left in the world that one can trust."

Then the swallow came:

"Tsee! Tsee!"he whistled and darted through the air on his long, pointed wings.

"Out with you, you silly flowers! Can't you see that Dame Spring has come?"

But the anemones had become careful. They just pushed their green wraps a little to one side and peeped out:

"One swallow does not make a summer," they said. "Where is your wife? You have only come to see if it's possible to live here and now you're trying to take us in. But we are not so stupid as all that. We know that, once we catch cold, we're done for."

"You're a pack of poltroons," said the swallow and sat down on the weathercock on the ranger's roof and looked out over the landscape.

But the anemones stood and waited and were very cold. One or two of them, who could not control their impatience, cast off their wraps in the sun. The cold at night killed them; and the story of their pitiful death went from flower to flower and aroused great consternation.

Then Dame Spring came, one delightfully mild and still night.

No one knows what she looks like, for no one has ever seen her. But all long for her and thank her and bless her. She goes through the wood and touches the flowers and the trees and they bud at once. She goes through the stables and unfastens the cattle and lets them out into the fields. She goes straight into men's hearts and gladdens them. She makes it difficult for the best-behaved boy to sit still on his bench at school and occasions a terrible lot of mistakes in the exercise-books.

But she does not do this all at once. She attends to her business night after night and comes direct to those who long for her most.

So it happened that, on the very night when she arrived, she went straight to the anemones, who stood in their green wraps and could no longer curb their impatience.

And one, two, three! There they stood in newly-ironed white frocks and looked so fresh and pretty that the starlings sang their finest songs for sheer joy at the sight of them.

"Oh, how lovely it is here!" said the anemones. "How warm the sun is! And how the birds are singing! It is a thousand times better than last year."

But they say this every year, so it doesn't count.

Now there were many others who went quite off their heads when they saw that the anemones were out. There was a schoolboy who wanted to have his summer holidays right away; and then there was the beech, who was highly offended:

"Aren't you coming to me soon, Dame Spring?" he said. "I am a much more important person than those silly anemones and really I can no longer control my buds."

"Coming, coming!" replied Dame Spring. "But you must give me a little time."

She went on through the wood. And, at every step, more anemones appeared. They stood in thick bevies around the roots of the beech and modestly bowed their round heads to the ground.

"Look up freely," said Dame Spring, "and rejoice in Heaven's bright sun. Your lives are but short, so you must enjoy them while they last."

The anemones did as she told them. They stretched themselves and spread their white petals to every side and drank as much sunshine as they could. They pushed their heads against one another and twined their stalks together and laughed and were wonderfully happy.

"Now I can wait no longer," said the beech and burst into leaf.

Leaf after leaf crept out of its green covering and spread out and fluttered in the wind. The whole green crown arched itself like a mighty roof above the earth.

"Good heavens, is it evening so soon?" asked the anemones, who thought that it had turned quite dark.

"No, this is death," said Dame Spring. "Now you're over. It's the same with you as with the best in this world. All must bud, blossom and die."

"Die?" cried some of the small anemones. "Must we die so soon?"

And some of the large anemones turned quite red in the face with anger and arrogance:

"We know all about it!" they said. "It's the beech that's killing us. He steals the sunshine for his own leaves and grudges us a single ray. He's a nasty, wicked thing."

They stood and scolded and wept for some days. Then Dame Spring came for the last time through the wood. She still had the oaks and some other querulous old fellows to visit:

"Lie down nicely to sleep now in the ground," she said to the anemones. "It's no use kicking against the pricks. Next year, I will come again and wake you to new life."

And some of the anemones did as she told them. But others continued to stick their heads in the air and grew up so ugly and lanky that they were horrid to look at:

"Fie, for shame!" they cried to the beech-leaves. "It's you that are killing us."

'FIE, FOR SHAME!' THEY CRIED TO THE BEECH-LEAVES. 'IT'S YOU THAT ARE KILLING US.'

But the beech shook his long boughs, so that the brown husks fell to the ground:

"Wait till autumn, you little blockheads," he said and laughed. "Then you'll just see."

The anemones could not understand what he meant. But, when they had stretched themselves as far as they could, they cracked in two and withered.

Summer was past and the farmer had carted his corn home from the field.

The wood was still green, but darker; and, in many places, yellow and red leaves appeared among the green ones. The sun was tired after his hot work during the summer and went to bed early.

At night, winter stole through the trees to see if his time would soon come. When he found a flower, he kissed her politely and said:

"Well, well, are you there still? I am glad to see you. Stay where you are. I am a harmless old man and wouldn't hurt a fly."

But the flower shuddered at his kiss and the bright dew-drops hanging from her petals froze to ice at the same moment.

Winter went oftener and oftener through the wood. He breathed upon the leaves, till they turned yellow, or upon the ground, till even the anemones, who lay below in the earth, waiting for Dame Spring to come again as she had promised, could feel his breath and shuddered right down to their roots:

"Oh dear, how cold it is!" they said to one another. "How ever shall we last through the winter? We are sure to die before it is over."

"Now my time has come," said winter. "Now I need no longer steal round like a thief in the night. From to-morrow, I shall look every one straight in the face and bite his nose and make his eyes run with tears."

At night, the storm broke loose.

"Let me see you make a clean sweep of things," said winter.

And the storm obeyed his orders. He tore howling through the wood and shook the branches till they creaked and broke. Any that were at all decayed fell down and those that held on had to twist and turn to every side.

"Away with all that finery!" howled the storm and tore off the leaves. "This is no time to dress yourselves up. Soon there will be snow on the branches: that's another story."

All the leaves fell terrified to the ground, but the storm did not let them lie in peace. He took them round the waist and waltzed with them over the field, high up in the air and into the wood again, swept them together into great heaps and scattered them once more to every side, just as the fit seized him.

Not until the morning did the storm grow weary and go down.

"Now you can have peace for *this* time," he said. "I am going down till we have our spring-cleaning. Then we can have another dance, if there are any of you left by then."

And the leaves went to rest and lay like a thick carpet over the whole earth.

The anemones felt that it had grown delightfully warm:

"I wonder if Dame Spring can have come yet?" they asked one another.

"I haven't my buds ready!" cried one of them.

"No more have I! No more have I!" exclaimed the others in chorus.

But one of them took courage and just peeped out above the ground.

"Good-morning!" cried the withered beech-leaves. "It's rather too early, young lady: if only you don't come to any harm!"

"Isn't that Dame Spring?" asked the anemone.

"Not just yet," replied the beech-leaves. "It's we, the green leaves you were so angry with in the summer. Now we have lost our brightness and have not much left to make a show of. We have enjoyed our youth and had our fling, you know. And now we are lying here and protecting all the little flowers in the ground against the winter."

"And meanwhile I am standing and freezing in my bare branches," said the beech, crossly.

The anemones talked about it down in the earth and thought it very nice:

"Those dear beech-leaves!" they said.

"Mind you remember it next summer, when I come into leaf," said the beech.

"We will, we will!" whispered the anemones.

For that sort of thing is promised, but the promise is never kept.

The WOOD and the HEATH

1

There was once a beautiful wood, filled with thousands of slender trunks and with singing and whispering in her dark tree-tops.

She was surrounded by field and meadow; and there the farmer had built his house. And field and meadow were good and green; and the farmer was hard-working and grateful for the crops which he brought home. But the wood stood like a lady of the manor, high above them all.

In the winter-time the fields lay flat and miserable, the meadow was merely one great lake with ice upon it and the farmer sat huddled in the chimney-corner; but the wood just stood straight and placid with her bare branches and let the weather storm and snow as it pleased. In the spring, both meadow and field turned green and the farmer came out and began to plough and sow. But the wood burst forth into so great a splendour that no one could hope to describe it: there were flowers at her feet and sunshine in her green tree-tops; the song of the birds echoed in even the smallest bush; and perfume and bright colours and gaiety reigned here and there and everywhere.

Now it happened, one summer's day, while the wood stood waving her branches, that she set eyes upon a funny brown thing which was spreading itself over the hills towards the west and which she had never seen before:

"What sort of fellow are you?" asked the wood.

"I am the heath," said the brown thing.

"I don't know you," said the wood, "and I don't like you: you are so ugly and black, you don't look like the field or the meadow or anything that I know. Can you bud into leaf? Can you blossom? Can you sing?"

"Indeed I can," said the heath. "In August, when your leaves begin to look dark and tired, my flowers will come out. Then I am purple, purple from end to end, and more beautiful than anything you have ever seen."

"You're a braggart!" said the wood; and the conversation dropped.

Next year, the heath had crept a little way down the hill, towards the wood. The wood saw this, but said nothing. She thought it beneath her dignity to talk to such an ugly fellow; but, in her heart of hearts, she was afraid. Then she made herself greener and prettier and looked as if there were nothing the matter.

But, every year, the heath came nearer. He had now covered all the hills and lay just outside the fence of the wood.

"Be off!" said the wood. "You annoy me. Take care you don't touch my fence!"

"I'm coming over your fence," said the heath. "I'm coming into you, to eat you up and destroy you."

Then the wood laughed till all her leaves quivered:

"So that's what you mean to do, is it?" she said. "If only you can manage it! I'm afraid that you will find me too big a mouthful. I daresay you think I'm a bit of a field or meadow, which one can walk over in a couple of strides. But I'm the most powerful and important person in the neighbourhood, you may as well know. I shall soon sing my song to you; then perhaps you will change your ways of thinking."

Then the wood began to sing. All the birds sang; and the flowers raised their heads and sang too. The smallest leaf hummed with the rest, the fox stopped in the middle of eating a fat chicken and beat time with his brush, the wind blew through the branches and played an organ accompaniment to the song of the wood:

>"Merrier meeting was never yet
>Than the festal wood discloses,
>When wood-ruff nestles by violet
>In a cluster of sweet wild roses.
>
>"Small birds in the brake fly up and down
>Nor ever a bird flies single
>And the woodman twines for his lass a crown
>Where berries and beech commingle.
>
>"Roe, fox and hare hold revel all,
>Thro' flowerage the wee worm glances;
>There great and small a-dancing fall
>And the sun up in Heaven dances."

"What do you say to that?" asked the wood.

The heath said nothing. But, next year, he came over the fence.

"Are you mad?" screamed the wood. "Why, I forbade you to cross the fence!"

"You are not my mistress," said the heath. "I am doing as I said I would."

Then the wood called the red fox and shook her branches so that a quantity of beech-mast fell upon him and remained hanging in his skin:

"Run across to the heath, Foxie, and scatter the beech-mast out there!" said the wood.

"Right you are!" said the fox and jogged away.

And the hare did the same and the marten and the mouse. And the crow lent a hand, for old acquaintance' sake, and the wind took hold and blew and shook the branches till the mast flew far out into the heath.

"That's it!" said the wood. "Now let's see what comes of *that*."

"Yes, let us!" said the heath.

A certain time passed and the wood grew green and withered and the heath spread more and more and they did not talk to each other. But, one fine spring day, tiny little new-born beeches and oaks peeped up from the ground round about in the heather.

"What do you say now?" asked the wood, triumphantly. "My trees shall grow year after year, till they become tall and strong. Then they shall close their tops over you: no sun shall shine, no rain shall fall upon you; and you shall die, as a punishment for your presumption."

But the heath shook his black twigs earnestly:

"You don't know me," he said. "I am stronger than you think. Your trees will never turn green in me. I have bound the earth under me as firm as iron and your roots can't go through it. Just wait till next year! Then the little fellows you are so pleased with will all be dead."

"You're lying," said the wood.

But she was frightened.

Next year, it happened as the heath had said. The little oaks and beeches died as one tree. And now a terrible time came for the wood. The heath spread more and more; on every side there was heather instead of violets and anemones. None of the young trees grew up, the bushes withered, the old trees began to die in their tops, and it was a general calamity.

"It's no longer at all pleasant in the wood," said the nightingale. "I think I shall build somewhere else."

"Why, there's hardly a decent tree left to live in!" said the crow.

"The ground has become so hard that it's no longer possible to dig one's self a proper hole and burrow," said the fox.

The wood was at her wits' end. The beech stretched his branches to the sky in an appeal for help and the oak wrung his in silent despair.

"Sing your song once more!" said the heath.

"I have forgotten it," replied the wood, gloomily. "And my flowers are withered and my birds have flown away."

"Then I will sing," said the heath.

And he sang:

> "A goodly song round the moorland goes
> When the sun in the east leaps clearer;
> And like blood or fire the heather glows
> As to autumn the woods draw nearer.
>
> "All day on the moor will the cotton-grass
> Weave its white, long bands together;
> And softly the snake and the adder pass
> Through the stems of the tufted heather.
>
> "On swinging tussock the lapwing leaps,
> Lark's note above plover's swelling,
> As the crook-backed cotter in silence creeps
> From his lonely moorland dwelling."

Gradually, as the years passed, things looked worse and worse for the wood. The heath spread farther and farther, until it reached the other end of the wood. The great trees died and toppled down as soon as the storm took a fair hold of them: then they lay and rotted and the heather grew over them. There were now only half a score of the oldest and strongest trees left; but they were altogether hollow and had quite thin tops.

"My time is over, I must die," said the wood.

"Well, I told you so beforehand," replied the heath.

But then the men and women began to grow very frightened at the way the heather was using the wood:

"Where am I to get timber for my workshop?" cried the joiner.

"Where am I to get sticks to put under my pot?" screamed the goodwife.

"Where, oh where, are we to get fuel in the winter?" sighed the old man.

"Where am I to stroll with my sweetheart in the spring?" asked the young one.

Then, when they had looked at the poor old trees for a bit, to see if there was anything to be done with them, they took their spades and mattocks and ran up the hills to where the heath began.

"You may as well save yourselves the trouble," said the heath. "I am not to be dug into."

"Alas, no!" sighed the wood; but she was so weak now that no one could hear what she said.

But they did not mind about that. They hewed and hewed right down through the hard shell. Then they carted earth into the holes and manured it; and then they planted some small trees. They tended them and put their faith in them and screened them against the east wind as well as they could.

And, year after year, the small trees grew. They stood like light, green spots in the middle of the black heather; and, when this had gone on for some time, a little bird came and built a nest in one of them.

"Hurrah!" shouted the men. "Now we've got a wood once more."

"No one can hold his own against men," said the heath. "The thing can't be helped. So we'll move on."

But of the old wood there still remained one tree, who had only one green twig in his top. Here a little bird settled and told of the new wood that was growing up on the hill yonder.

"Thank Heaven!" said the old wood. "What one can't do one's self one must leave to the children. If only they're good for something! They look so thin!"

"I daresay you were thin yourself once," said the bird.

The old wood said nothing to this, for at that very moment she was finished; and so, of course, my story is finished too.

SOMEWHERE IN THE WOOD

1

Somewhere in the wood, quite close to one another, lived a little company of good friends.

There was the sheep's-scabious, who looked as if she had something on her head, but had not, and the bell-flower, who was so blue and modest. There was the maiden-pink, meeker and redder and gentler than any, and a few blades of grass, who were nice and green, but poor and quite grateful if one as much as looked at them. Then there was some moss, which grew on the old stump of a tree and kept to itself, and there was the hazel-bush, who was the finest of them all, both because he was so big and, especially, because the linnet had built his nest in him.

The friends never had a word.

They all minded their own business and did not stand in one another's way. In the evening, when the day's work was done, they listened to the linnet's song. Or else there would be a creaking in the hazel-bush's branches; and that was quite as uncanny as a regular ghost-story. Or else the blades of grass would just whisper softly and nonsensically; but that also is nice to listen to sometimes when you are tired and have nothing on your conscience.

If anything joyful happened to any one of the friends, they all rejoiced. When the maiden-pink and the bell-flower budded, the hazel-bush offered his congratulations, the linnet struck his longest trill and the blades of grass appointed a deputation and bowed respectfully to the ground and each shed a dewy tear of emotion. When the little linnets crept out of the egg, all the friends were as happy as if they themselves had had children.

From out of the wood came the whistling and singing of many birds, but this did not concern the friends. Sometimes a roe would come bounding or a fox sneaking along; and once a frightened hare hid under the hazel-bush, while the guns banged all around and the dogs gave tongue. They would talk about an event like this for days together. But then they lapsed into quietude again; and time wore on to summer.

Then, one morning, the maiden-pink felt strangely unwell.

Her stalks and leaves were slack and she had a regular pain in her roots. Her flowers were so queer and loose, she thought.

When she complained of not being well, the sheep's-scabious and the bell-flower said that it was just the same with them. So did the blades of grass, but that did not count, for they always agreed with any one they were talking to. The moss said nothing, but that did not signify either, for nobody asked him.

"We want rain," said the hazel-bush. "There's nothing else the matter. It doesn't affect me yet, but I suppose it will. You are so short and slender; that's why you feel it first."

The blades of grass nodded and thought that this was remarkably well said on the part of the hazel-bush. The others hung their heads. The linnet sang as best he could to cheer the sick friends.

But sick they were and sick they remained; and it grew worse every day.

"I think I'm dying," said the maiden-pink.

The blades of grass observed, most politely, that they were already half-dead. The hazel-bush was not feeling well either and the linnet thought the air so heavy that he was not at all inclined to sing.

And, while they were talking about all this, towards the evening, they heard the same complaint in the whispering that came from the great wood, in the bell of the stag and the bay of the fox and the croak of the frog and the squeak of the mouse in her hole. The ranger and the farmer went past and talked about it; they looked up at the bright sky and shook their heads:

"We shall have no rain to-morrow either," said the ranger. "My small trees are dying."

"And my corn is being blighted," said the farmer.

Next morning, the friends became seriously alarmed when they looked at one another.

They were hardly recognizable, so ill did they appear, with yellow, hanging leaves and faded flowers and dry roots. Only the moss looked as usual.

"Don't you feel anything?" asked the hazel-bush.

"Yes, I do," said the moss. "But it doesn't show in me. I might lie here and be dead for a whole month and all the time look as if I were alive and well. I can't help it."

"I shall go up and look for a cloud," said the linnet.

And he went up in the air, so high that he was quite lost to the others, and he came back and said that there was a cloud far away in the west.

"Ask him to come," said the bell-flower, in a faint voice.

And the linnet flew up again and came back presently with the sad answer that the cloud could not:

"He would like to," said the linnet. "He is tired of hanging up there with all that rain. But he has to wait till the wind comes for him."

"Good-bye," said the maiden-pink. "And thank you for the pleasant time we have had together. I can hold out no longer."

'GOOD-BYE,' SAID THE MAIDEN-PINK.

And then she died. All the friends looked at one another in dismay:

"We must get hold of the wind," said the hazel-bush, who had more life left in him than the others. "Else it will be all up with every one of us."

Next morning early, the wind came stealing along. He came quite slowly, for he too was tired of the intolerable dry heat; but he had to go his rounds for all that.

"Dear Wind," said the sheep's-scabious. "Bring us a little cloud, or we shall all be dead."

"There is no cloud," said the wind.

"That's not true, Wind," said the linnet. "There's a beautiful grey cloud far away in the west."

"Re-ally?" said the wind. "Ah ... I happen to be the east wind just now, so I can't help you."

"Turn round, dear Wind, and bring us the cloud," asked the bell-flower, civilly. "You can blow wherever you please and we shall be grateful to you as long as we live."

"You will earn the thanks of the whole community," said the hazel-bush.

"The whole community," whispered the blades of grass.

"I daresay," said the wind. "But I am not what you take me for. You believe that I am my own master, because I come shifting and shifting about and sometimes blow gently and sometimes hard and am sometimes mild and sometimes keen. But I am merely a dog that comes when his master calls."

"Who is your master then?" asked the linnet. "I will go to him, even if he lives at the end of the earth."

"Ah ... if *that* were enough!" said the wind. "My master is the sun. I run my race at his behest. When he shines really strong anywhere, than I go up with the warm air and fetch cold air from somewhere else and fly with it along the earth. Whether it be east or west does not concern me."

"I don't understand it," said the linnet.

"I don't understand it either," said the wind. "But I *do* it!"

Then he went down. And the friends stood and hung their heads and were at their wits' end:

"There is nothing for it but to die," said the sheep's-scabious.

"If I have lived through the winter," said the hazel-bush, "I suppose I can stand this. But it's very hard."

And the bell-flower and the sheep's-scabious, who had never lived through the winter, wondered if it could really be worse than this. And the linnet dreamt of the south, where *he* spent the winter; and the blades of grass had quite thrown up the game.

"Can't your branches reach up to the sun?" asked the sheep's-scabious of the hazel-bush.

"Can't you fly up to the sun?" asked the bell-flower of the linnet.

But that they could not do; and the days passed and the wretchedness increased. It was quite silent in the wood. Not a bird chirped, the fox stayed in his hole, the stag lay in the shade and gasped, with his tongue hanging out of his mouth, and the trees stood with drooping branches, as though they were at a funeral.

Then the bell-flower rang all her bells, as if to ring in death over the wood. It sounded quite still and weak and nevertheless rose high in the air like a prayer:

"My blue bells chime for the rain to fall
In dusty and desolate places,
Where buds that should shine and be fragrant all
Are pining with pallid faces."

It is not easy to know who heard it; and none of the friends said a word. But, at that moment, they all plainly heard some one speak and then they all knew that it was the sun, whom the hazel-bush could not reach with his branches and whom the linnet could not fly to, but who had heard the bell-flower's plaints:

"I shine as I must and not as I please; and I cannot help you. I am bound to go my course round another sun, who is a thousand times larger and better than I. I cannot swerve a foot's breadth from my road; I cannot send down a single ray according to my own wishes."

"I don't understand it," said the hazel-bush.

"I don't understand it either," said the sun. "But I *do* it."

"And I understand that it is all up with a poor sheep's-scabious," said the sheep's-scabious and died then and there.

Then night came and all thought that it would be their last.

But, suddenly, the bell-flower raised her aching head and listened.

She thought she heard a sound as when a drop falls ... now came another ... it smacked down upon a leaf ... and another ... and another....

They all woke up, while the rain poured in torrents.

The poor blades of grass stood up, the unhappy moss took fresh courage. The linnet began to sing, though it was a dark night. The hazel-bush shook with delight, until he nearly shook the linnet's young out of the nest.

Everything round about in the wood revived. The night was full of happiness. The ranger and the farmer rose from their beds and met in the rain and shook each other by the hand with glad eyes.

It rained the whole night and the day after and the next night and one day more. Sometimes it rained gently and sometimes hard. The ground drank all the water with a thirsty mouth and the roots sucked it greedily out of the ground and leaves and flowers unfolded and stood erect and blithe on slender stalks.

Then came the third day, with sunshine and a blue sky and life and merriment in the wood.

"Well," said the wind and came darting along as though he had never been tired in his life, "do you see, I brought you the rain?"

"Well," said the cloud, who drifted high above, in a light, white summer suit, "did you see how I came with the rain?"

"Well," said the sun and laughed, rounder and warmer than ever, "so you got what you asked me for!"

The friends looked at one another in surprise. But, a little way off, sat the red fox, with his ugly, clever face:

"That's the sort of people they are," he said. "When you ask them for something, they're not at home. But they never forget to call for thanks!"

THE COUSINS

A Story of the House-mouse, the Wood-mouse, the Field-mouse, The Black Rat and the Brown Rat.

1

The house-mouse went about quietly, minding her business.

She lived in the forester's house that lay just on the skirt of the forest, so that there were woods on one side and fields on the other. She had a comfortable home behind the wainscot in the forester's dining-room, right under the window. And the window looked out on the woods; and then down at the bottom of the wall there was a very tiny hole, which the house-mouse was just able to squeeze through, so that she could slip into the woods and home again whenever she pleased.

In this way, the house-mouse had a very enjoyable time; and she had a good time also with regard to the people she lived with. True, the forester was a grumpy sort of man, who could not hear the word "mouse" mentioned without flying into a rage. But he was a very old man and the house was managed by his daughter. She never forgot the house-mouse; and this came of a meeting that once took place between the two. One morning, you must know, the young lady went to the sideboard to get out the sugar for her father's coffee. And there sat the mouse in the sugar-basin. She had forgotten the time and gone to sleep. And there she *was*!

Of course, she was terribly frightened; and it was worse still when the girl put out her hand over the sugar-basin, as if to catch her:

"So there you are, Mousie!" she said. "I *thought* it was you that was after my sugar! Apart from that, you're a nice little thing. But you needn't go shaking so terribly in your little grey shoes, for, I assure you, I have not the least intention of doing you any harm. Perhaps you have little children, who would starve if you didn't come home to them. So I'll let you go. But, on the other hand, it will never do for you to go stealing our sugar. So, when you get down to the floor, run straight to your hole. I don't know where it is, but, when I find out, I will put a piece of sugar on the floor outside it, every evening before I go to bed. And then I will look for the hole through which you got into the sideboard and stop it up; and then we shall be friends."

When she had made this speech, which was much handsomer than the speeches which mice are accustomed to hear from human beings, she put the terrified mouse down on the floor. The mouse at once scudded across the room and disappeared in her hole under the wainscoting.

"So that's where you live," said the forester's daughter. "That's all right. Now you will see I shall remember my promise."

In the evening she put a lump of sugar there and she did so every evening before she went to bed. And, every morning, the mouse had fetched the sugar. And, when, one day, she heard a squeaking behind the wainscot, she guessed that the little mouse had now got children; and, from that day, she put two lumps of sugar for her every evening.

The mouse, therefore, could not complain of the people she lived with and no more she did. Add to this that the only cat that the forester's house contained was an enormous old ginger tom who could no longer either see or hear. He had been there in the forester's wife's day. She was dead now. And, as she had been fond of him, he was allowed to live and eat the bread of charity in the forester's house, though he was no longer of the least use. And, as he could not tolerate other and younger cats, there was no other cat in the place, which of course was a great source of joy to the mouse, who often ran right under the old ginger tomcat's nose, without his noticing her.

One day, the mouse was sitting outside the hole that led to the wood. It was in the month of August and it was warm and pleasant and she sat basking in the sun with the greatest enjoyment, the more so as she had just given birth to seven blind children, which is no joke, as any mother will tell you. And, as she sat there, the wood-mouse came out of her house under the root of the beech.

"Good-afternoon, cousin," said the house-mouse.

"The same to you, cousin," said the wood-mouse.

"A fine sunny day," said the house-mouse.

"The same to you, cousin," said the wood-mouse.

When they had greeted each other in this fashion, they sat and looked at each other for a little while. The house-mouse moved her big ears to and fro; and the wood-mouse did the same, out of courtesy, but her ears were not nearly so big. On the other hand, she had more hairs in her tail than her cousin, so that pretty well made up for the ears. Then the house-mouse said:

"Life is lovely."

"Do you think so, cousin?" said the wood-mouse.

And she looked as though she were of a very different opinion, but too polite to say so outright.

"Yes, I do, cousin," replied the house-mouse. "I have just got my last seven youngsters off my hands. And every evening the young mistress puts a piece of sugar outside my hole for me. And the forester and the cat are both so old that they positively can't see when I run through the room. And yesterday an old lady arrived whose name is Petronella. And she's as frightened of me as though she were a mouse and I a cat. When she sees me, she screams and gathers up her skirts and jumps on a chair, old as she is. This amuses the young lady who gives me the sugar immensely, so I like doing it. And, for the matter of that, I needn't even trouble to come out. This morning, I was sitting in my hole while they were drinking tea. Then my young mistress cried, 'There's the mouse!' and in a jiffy Aunt Petronella was up on the chair, though I wasn't there at all. I tell you, it's great fun."

"I daresay, cousin," said the wood-mouse. "And I'm very glad indeed that you've such a good time."

"And haven't you just as good a time?" asked the house-mouse. "Living in the green wood and hearing the birds sing all day long? No cat and no mouse-traps?"

"Yes, it's all right about the birds," said the wood-mouse. "And about the cats too. But you mustn't think on that account, cousin, that this is a sort of paradise. I hear very little of the birds down where I live; and I may as well admit that I don't bother my head about them. Besides, there are one or two awkward customers among them, such as the crow, for instance, and the rook and the jackdaw, who all belong to the same family. Not to speak of the stork and the buzzard, for whom a wood-mouse is a mere mouthful."

"Yes, I know," said the house-mouse. "Well, we all have our worries. And, at any rate, you don't have the cat. She's the trickiest of the lot."

"Is she?" said the wood-mouse. "Well, you may be right. But we have the fox out here, you know, who is pretty cunning, in addition to the marten and the polecats, who are the blood-thirstiest animals that you can think of. No, taken all round, believe me, it's not so pleasant to be a wood-mouse. And it's very likely that what is your good fortune is just my misfortune!"

"Why, how can that be, cousin?" asked the house-mouse. "I can't understand it and I should be sorry to think so."

"Well, you see, it's not a thing that *you* can help," said the wood-mouse. "Heaven forbid! You have always been a first-rate cousin; I don't deny it for a moment. But I expect the reason why you have a good time is that you live with an old gentleman like your forester. The natural consequence is a cat and a sweet young daughter who gives you sugar. Perhaps it would not be so pleasant for you if the forester died and a new one came who was younger. His wife might be too fond of her sugar to care to give you any. His children might set traps for you and torture you. And he might have a young cat, who would get her claws into you and eat you."

"You are very likely right," said the house-mouse. "All the more reason why I should value my good fortune while it lasts. But, all the same, I can't understand how my good fortune can be your misfortune."

THERE SAT THE MOUSE IN THE SUGAR BASIN.

"Oh, it's not so difficult to understand as all that!" said the wood-mouse. "You see, when a forester is very old, he looks after the wood badly. He is no longer able to shoot and, taken all round, he knows nothing about what goes on out of doors. The result is that there is such an immense number of foxes and martens and polecats and buzzards out here that one of us can hardly stir from her hole without risking her life. Now, if a new and young forester were to come, you can easily understand what a change that would make in things."

"Oh yes!" said the house-mouse. "Now I understand! But tell me, cousin, don't you think the new forester would also go for the mice, if he could? It seems to me I have heard the old one say that the mice are the wood's worst enemies. And it must be the wood-mice he means. For I don't know of any harm that I do to the wood."

The wood-mouse set up her tail and shook her little head sorrowfully:

"Cousin," she said, "you have touched me on my very sorest point."

"I am really sorry, cousin," said the house-mouse. "But it appears to me that it was you who began to talk about it."

"So it was, cousin," said the wood-mouse. "And we don't do any good by holding our tongues. You see, cousin, there is a great deal of wickedness in this world; and we have to put up with it. But it's pretty hard when it comes from one's relations."

"That's true, cousin," said the house-mouse. "Are there really any of your relations who do you any harm?"

"Harm?" said the wood-mouse. "I daresay that those of whom I'm thinking don't think of doing me any harm. But they do so for this reason, that they behave themselves in such a way that we have to suffer for it. And, as far as relationship is concerned, they are your relations as well as mine."

"But who are they, cousin?" asked the house-mouse. "Tell me, quickly. I have no notion of whom you're thinking."

"I'm thinking of the field-mouse," said the wood-mouse, with a deep sigh.

The house-mouse was silent for a moment, out of respect for the other's emotion. And presently the wood-mouse began to speak of her own accord:

"The field-mouse is our cousin, cousin, our own first cousin. There's no denying the fact. But I must confess that I think she does the family no credit. She is preposterously greedy. And her absurd gluttony injures all of us. The tale is that the mice have done it. And so they have. But who thinks of asking which mouse it is that has done it? Is it you? No. You mind your own business indoors, in the house. Of course, you nibble at a ham or a loaf or an old cheese or anything that comes your way. That's only reasonable. One has to live; and goodness knows what might be said of the way in which human beings get their food, if the matter were looked into."

"What you say is an absolute fact," said the house-mouse. "I have often thought, when I have been nibbling at a ham, that, if I was a thief, then the forester, whose ham it was, was neither more nor less than a murderer. Well ... and then they have the cat and the mouse-trap and all the rest of their cunning, so they're all right. A poor mouse has to think very hard and to risk her life pretty well every hour of the day if she is to provide herself with food."

"Just so," said the wood-mouse. "It's not you. Then who is it? Is it I? No, I mind my business as you mind yours. Of course, I take nuts and beech-mast and acorns, when they fall; and I admit that I am a regular whale for fir-cones. That fresh fir-seed is about the nicest thing I know. So I gnaw the cones in two and eat the seeds; and then they are gone when the forester wants them to sow firs with. But that is only reasonable. I must live as well as he and there are quite enough firs in the world. And I won't deny I may eat a bit of root once in a way, in the spring, when the roots are quite fresh. But what then? The forester himself is fond of vegetables, so he really need not grudge me a few."

"Certainly not," said the house-mouse. "You are quite right, cousin. You only do what we all do."

"Thank you for that kind word, cousin," said the wood-mouse. "I think it's only fair. Well, just as he has the cat and the mouse-trap for you, if you become too indiscreet, so he has the fox and the crow and the polecat and the marten and the stork and, above all, the owl for me. You can't imagine what a terribly cunning enemy the owl is. One simply can't hear him flying. One can't see him either, for he only comes at night and his colours are dark. And they all see as well at night as an ordinary body does in broad daylight. And he has all these fellows gratis. The cat and the trap he has to buy. But his forest-police he gets for nothing."

"That's true," said the house-mouse.

"Therefore it's not I either," said the wood-mouse. "It's not you and it's not I. Shall I tell you who it is? It's our cousin, the field-mouse. The mice have done it, the story goes. And who are the mice? It's the field-mouse. But he is not the only one who has to be prosecuted and punished. Any one bearing the name of mouse is mercilessly and ruthlessly struck down. People are so stupid. They can see no difference. And I don't know how to teach them any better. It's too bad!"

"But, cousin," said the house-mouse, "you haven't told me yet what the field-mouse does that the rest of us are blamed for. It must be something shocking to upset you so."

"Indeed, the forester is more upset than I am," said the wood-mouse. "And I don't deny that he has every reason to be. You see, just round the corner is a beautiful, green forest-glade. The deer come out here and graze, early in the morning, and they drink from a brook that runs through the glade. It makes a charming picture. I have seen it myself on many a fine summer morning, when I have come home rejoicing at my good luck in escaping the owl and the other ruffians. Well, the forester is particularly fond of the glade, because he uses it for his horses. He makes hay there. And it's the loveliest forest-hay that you can imagine."

"Yes, I know," said the house-mouse. "I saw him carting hay into the barn last year."

"Yes, but there will be no hay this year," said the wood-mouse. "You see, cousin, some time ago the glade began to wither and turn yellow. It became yellower and yellower every day. The keeper came and told the forester. They were out the other day looking at it. Then they discovered that all the grass-roots were eaten up or gnawed through. They were able to roll up the whole grassy surface like a carpet; and they did so. I was sitting at the edge of the wood myself, looking on. The grass was gone and the hay and everything; and the field-mouse had done it."

"Our cousin must be awfully hungry," said the house-mouse. "Or perhaps he has a big family."

"Both," said the wood-mouse. "Both. He is awfully greedy and he always has the house full of children. Well, that doesn't concern us: it's his affair. But, when those silly men mix us up in it, lump us all together with Cousin Field-Mouse and persecute us and kill us for what he has done, I tell you, cousin, then it *does* concern us!"

"That's true," said the house-mouse.

They sat on; and neither spoke. It was getting on towards evening; and both of them had to go to work when it grew dark. Summer was almost over, so the wood-mouse had begun to collect her winter-stores. She did not lie torpid like the hedgehog or the bat and she could not fly to Africa like the stork and the swallow, so she had to have her store-room filled, if she did not wish to suffer want. She had already collected a good deal of beech-mast. But the nuts were not ripe yet and, if she took them before they were ripe, they were no good to her.

And the house-mouse also chose night for going to the larder. Even though her young mistress did nothing to her, nevertheless she dared not be over-impudent, but always waited until she was certain that she would not be disturbed.

"Yes," said the wood-mouse, "we must start toiling for our daily bread again. At any rate, you are better off than I, cousin, for the present, as you don't have the winter to think about. You're snug indoors, close to the forester's larder."

"I am," said the house-mouse. "And there is almost more in the larder in the winter than in the summer."

"Yes, yes," said the wood-mouse. "Well, good-bye, cousin: if you meet the field-mouse, be sure to tell him what I said. I always stand by my word. And, if you can contrive some means of letting the forester know that there's a difference between mice and mice, so much the better. You are nearer to him than we are."

"Wait a little longer, cousin," said the house-mouse. "After all, it's not dark enough yet for you to work; and I never go to the larder before my young lady has cleared away after supper. I've been thinking of what you were saying about the field-mouse and most of all of what you said about relations doing harm. For, you see, properly speaking, it's just the same indoors."

"You don't say so!" said the wood-mouse. "I should never have thought that the field-mouse had the impudence to come in to you. I must hear more about that. Then it's in the garden that he is?"

"No," said the house-mouse. "It's not the field-mouse at all. I don't know anything about him. I have never even set eyes on him, that I know of. But, as we know, we have another big cousin, called the rat."

"I have heard a little about him," said the wood-mouse. "But I have never seen him. Is he of the same kind as the field-mouse?"

"He is much worse," said the house-mouse. "To begin with, he is so awfully big. I should say he is as big as five fat mice put together. He is quite black, with a long, scaly tail and small ears. He has horrid teeth and a long tongue. And he is greedier than I know how to tell you. He plays just the same part in the house that the field-mouse does among your people. And what happens to you happens to me: I often get blamed for his mean tricks. Just think, one day last year, he bit the odd man in the nose as he lay sleeping one afternoon in the hayloft. He took quite a little bit of flesh, so that the man had to go to the doctor and walk about with a bandage for many days."

"That's horrid," said the wood-mouse. "And it's quite unlike a mouse's nature. We are not beasts of prey, that I *do* know. Do you really believe he's our cousin?"

"He is indeed," said the house-mouse. "I know it; and there's no mistaking it either, when you see him. He is the perfect image of a mouse, though he is clumsier. But he is a disgrace to the family; and that's a fact. And fancy what happened. I was just outside the larder: I have a little waiting-hole there, where I sit and wait when I come too early and when my young lady is still in the kitchen. And I was sitting there on the evening it happened; I had been sitting there some time, for it looked as though my young lady was never going. I must tell you she was waiting for the odd man, who had ridden off to the doctor with his nose. He was to have his supper when he came home. He arrived at last and, while he sat there eating his food and talking to the young lady about what had happened, she said that those rats were most disgusting animals and ought to be exterminated in every possible way. 'Yes,' she said. 'I can't abide them for the life of me. And then they are so hideous to look at. They look quite wicked. But I must intercede for the dear little mice. I love them. I have a tiny one, whom I know well and am ever so fond of. I caught her one day in the sugar-basin, the little thief!'

"'And didn't you kill her, miss?' asked the man.

"'Why, no!' she said. 'I never thought of such a thing! I let her run away to her hole and now, every evening, I put a lump of sugar outside the hole for her. And, every morning, when I come to the dining-room, it's gone. But you mustn't tell father, Jens.' Jens promised that he would not. But he went on to say that mice and rats were one and the same kind of vermin all together and ought to be exterminated. Then the forester came in and agreed with Jens; and nothing that his daughter said to the contrary was of any use. The forester said that he would see and get a regular rat-catcher out here, who would lay poison for the lot of us. And all this is surely not my fault, but is due to that disgusting rat, who bit Jens in the nose. It is really no joke having a reprobate like that in the family, disgracing one's good name."

"No," said the wood-mouse, "that's what I say. And how are we to inform the human beings of their mistake? I know no way of obtaining speech with them. Well, good-bye, cousin, and *au revoir*."

"Good-bye, cousin, and *au revoir* to you," said the house-mouse.

Then the one went out into the wood, to forage for the winter, and the other into her young lady's larder.

Some time after, a great, big packing-case of groceries arrived at the forester's house from Copenhagen. Here ought to be enough to last all through the winter, the forester thought. And he belonged to the old school, who laid in their stores once a year at a fixed time and no other, and he had done so from the first year when he and his wife came to live in the forester's house.

Now the packing-case was so big that the young lady and the odd man were at their wits' end to know what to do with it. It could not go into the house, for there was no door wide enough to admit it. It could not remain out in the yard either, for the young lady could not unpack it that day, as she happened to be very busy bottling plums. And, of course, she had to be present herself: there was no question about that. And it was beginning to look like rain. The forester said that it would certainly rain that night. He could feel it in his left shoulder, which was a barometer that never went wrong.

"Can't we tumble it into the barn?" said the odd man. "It can stay there as long as need be, without hurting."

So they tumbled it into the barn. And there it stood, in a corner. It remained there for five days. But, on the very first night, while the rain came pouring down, as the forester's left shoulder had foretold, a shocking thing happened.

Suddenly, then and there, a queer sound began to come from the end of the packing-case that was nearest to the corner of the barn. It was a sort of gnawing and creaking, as though there were an animal inside. And it was soon proved that that was what it was. For, when the gnawing had lasted some time, a great, fat, brown rat came out of the case.

The moment she appeared, a quantity of sugar came pouring over her. The rat did not so much as touch the sugar. She had had enough of that inside the case. She began at once to gnaw a hole in the floor, at a place where the boards were rather rotten, so that it was an easy job. The hole was soon ready and there was plenty of room for a family of rats under the boards. The rat immediately began to collect straw and took it down with her.

When she had finished her work, she stopped and looked the house-mouse straight in the face.

"Who in the name of wonder are you?" asked the house-mouse. "You have mousy ways and, if you were black, I should say you were a rat."

"I am a rat," said the other. "Rats were black in the old days. The fashion now is to be brown. Black rats are quite out of date and are of no use to-day."

"Oh, really!" said the house-mouse, circumspectly. "Well, I live out here in the country, and know nothing of what goes on in the great world beyond. Allow me to introduce myself. I am the house-mouse."

"You needn't tell me that," said the rat. "I have seen many of your sort at Copenhagen. But what are you doing out here on the threshing-floor? I thought you kept to the kitchen and the larder."

"So I do, as a rule," said the house-mouse. "But I am free to go where I please. And I can come through the kitchen-drain without getting wet. For it's raining terribly, let me tell you."

"What of that?" said the rat. "Are you afraid of a little water? The more the better. I can swim like a fish, you know. I once swam across the harbour at Copenhagen; and, as a matter of fact, I don't feel well unless I have a little swim every day. I hope there's a decent gutter here?"

"Ugh, yes, a horrid broad one!" said the mouse. "But I always go round it. I don't set foot in the kitchen-drain either, except when it's dry. To-day, I came to get a bit out of the new case of groceries. I heard my young lady say that it had arrived. And generally there is a bit here and there outside to pick up."

"Certainly it has arrived," said the rat. "I ought to know, seeing that I came with it."

"Did you come with the case?" cried the house-mouse, in surprise.

"I did," said the rat. "I was down at the bottom when they began to pack it. It was half-dark, so they couldn't see me; and, of course, I did not make the slightest sound and did not dare to move, or else they would have discovered me and killed me. So gradually they packed everything on the top of me: sugar and coffee and tea and cinnamon and chocolate and starch and all sorts of groceries, until the case was full up. Then on with the lid and away with us to the station."

"That must have been a nice journey," said the house-mouse, licking her lips.

"It was," said the rat. "In a way. The fare was good enough and ready to hand, as you can see, and no one to share it with and no one to disturb you. But the tiresome side of the business was that I had just been married and was soon to have my babies. So I was particularly frightened lest they should arrive during the journey. However, it went pretty well and we escaped all right, as you see, because the case was not unpacked at once. Well, even if it had been, I daresay I should have managed to jump past them. But it's better as it is. I have fixed up a nice home for myself here, under the floor of the barn, and the youngsters may come as soon as they like. Would you care to see where I live?"

"Thank you," said the mouse. "I should prefer first to see a little of that delicious sugar running about. What a lot of it there is!"

"Eat away," said the rat. "There's plenty of it. I'll stand treat. But I may as well tell you that later on, when I am properly settled, you and I had better keep to our own parts. I mean, of course, it might happen that I should pop across to the larder, when I feel inclined and have occasion to. But I strongly advise you not to come here. And you must be particularly careful to avoid me when I'm hungry. I can't answer for what might happen if I met you."

"Well, you would never eat me!" said the mouse, sitting and licking the sugar. "Goodness me, how delicious this is!"

"Of course, I should eat you," replied the rat. "Up at Copenhagen, one day, we ate a kitten."

"A kitten?"

The mouse was so frightened that she stopped licking altogether.

"Yes, certainly," said the rat. "It was quite simple; and not one of us had the stomach-ache. That fear of the cats is very much overdone. They can do nothing, so long as you eat them while they are small."

The house-mouse stared at her in dismay:

"Cousin," she said, "you're terrible. I'm afraid of you."

"That's very sensible of you," said the rat. "And you mustn't call me cousin. I have never troubled about distant connections; and it would only make it unpleasant if I were to eat you one day. But, for the present, I have had my fill, as I said; so you run no risk."

The house-mouse then visited the rat in her new home, which she thought ever so nice, though a little too large from a mouse's point of view. After that, she said good-bye and went back to her own place. But, during the next few days, she came across to the barn every night and had her share of the good things in the packing-case. The rat gnawed the hole bigger, so that more came rushing out, always on the side turned towards the corner, where no one could suspect it. The floor overflowed with dainties; and they ate away like anything. On the fourth day, the rat had her children, seven fine little ones.

"They look pretty enough to be mice," said the house-mouse.

"Heaven forbid!" said the rat. "If they don't become proper rats soon, I will eat them without hesitation."

That night, the house-mouse took a large piece of cinnamon across with her; for she had heard her young lady say that the case must be opened shortly, so she was able to calculate that the fun would soon be over.

"Aren't you afraid of being discovered?" she asked the rat.

"A rat is never afraid," replied the rat. "If she were afraid, my good girl, she would not be a rat."

"It must be strange to feel like that," said the house-mouse. "A house-mouse is always afraid. If she were not afraid, I expect she would not be a mouse."

"Very likely," said the rat. "But you had better go now. And remember our arrangement that, when the case is gone, it's all over with friendship and relationship and the rest of it."

"All right," said the mouse. "I shall make a point of keeping away. But then you must always remember that it was you who bit the hole in the case and stood treat with all this. If you hadn't come, I should only have licked a bit on the outside, as usual."

"You're a fool!" said the rat. "Good-bye."

4

The next day—it was ten o'clock in the morning: they remembered it many years after at the forester's—the young lady and the odd man came across to the barn to unpack the case. The man rolled it across the threshing-floor; and, as soon as it was outside, they saw what had happened. Everything rolled out helter-skelter and higgledy-piggledy: coffee, tea, cinnamon, spices, sugar-candy, all without end and all mixed up together and spoilt. There was not a bag but had a hole in it.

They thought, at first, that it was the grocer's fault for packing the things badly; and the young lady was so angry with him that he would have been very much hurt if he had heard all the things that she said. But then they discovered the hole in one of the corners and soon saw that some one had been there and wrought havoc.

"There must have been rats here," said the forester's daughter. "There's no question about it: there have been rats here."

"There are no rats left in the place," said the man. "We killed the last a fortnight ago. And all their holes are stopped with broken glass; and we laid poison among their tracks; and every bit of poison is eaten up; so you can be easy in your mind, miss, about the rats. They are done with. But some one has been here, that is sure enough. And I am certain it's that artful mouse whom you spoil by giving her sugar every evening."

"Never!" said the young lady. "My little mouse could not possibly be such an ungrateful wretch as that."

The odd man stuck to his opinion and she stuck to hers. The forester came and, of course, sided with the man. They were all three angry and most of all the forester. For a new case had to be written for and he would have to pay for it. And so he resolved that, this time, the rat-catcher should be sent for in earnest. The odd man suggested a new cat, but that the forester would not hear about, so long as the old one lived.

In the meantime, they rescued what they could and the young lady carried the things into the larder, right past the nose of the mouse, who was sitting in her hole:

"They are speaking harm of you, my dear little Mouse," she said. "And now there's a horrid rat-catcher coming, who will try to hurt you, if he can. But I'm sure it was not you who did it and I will see if I can help you."

As she spoke, she saw a piece of cinnamon which the mouse had left lying outside her hole. She took it up and examined it and, as they had not a scrap of cinnamon in the house, she knew at once that the mouse had been at the case after all. She was so much upset that she cried. For she felt that life was not worth living if she could not even trust her own dear little mouse to whom she had been so kind:

"For shame, for shame!" she cried. "See how deceitful you are. But you shall have no more sugar from me, you can be sure of that."

But the mouse sat in her hole and cried also. First because of the sugar which she was not to get any longer. Next because of the rat-catcher who was to come. And then because of the kind young lady, who was so unjust to her. For, though she had taken the cinnamon, it was not she who had gnawed a hole in the packing-case. And it was too much to expect of an ordinary, plain little mouse that she should say no when a rat invited her to such a feast. But she couldn't talk to her young lady and explain it to her; and so, of course, she would never get any more sugar in future.

Over in the barn, the rat lay snug and warm in her nest. Her young ones grew from day to day. By the time that they had been a month in the world, they were big, greedy rats who did credit to their mamma and scooted about in every direction.

"You were right, miss, there are rats here," said the odd man. "But they are brown ones, who are much worse than the black ones that were here before. I am half-inclined to believe that they came in the packing-case from Copenhagen. I have never been there, but my cousin, who is in service in the town, tells me that there are an awful lot of them."

"It's quite possible," said the forester's daughter. "But I know that my little mouse had something to do with it; so I don't defend her any longer and I don't give her any sugar either."

"That's right," said the odd man. "For rats and mice are one and the same thing; and they are noxious vermin, the whole lot of them. If we let them get the upper hand of us, they would soon eat us out of house and home."

"The rat-catcher is coming on Thursday," said the forester. "Jens must drive to the station to fetch him. And the young man from the School of Forestry, who is to be my assistant, is coming by the same train. I am too old now and can't look after the wood as I ought to."

5

More time passed and it was winter.

All the birds that ever went away had gone. The leaves had fallen from the trees; it had frozen and it had snowed. The wood had been quite white and beautiful and then again sloppy and wretched to look at, for that's what winter is in Denmark. The forester seldom went out into the wood since his assistant had arrived. He generally sat in his warm room, in his old arm-chair, making up his accounts and thinking of the old days when he was young and active and never bothered whether it was warm or cold. He was also very fond of talking about that time. And, although he had talked about it more than once or twice before, they forgave him, because he was so old, and listened to him patiently.

Jens attended to his work, which was not very heavy in the winter. The forester's daughter spent her time between the kitchen and the larder. The rat-catcher had been and gone, after doing his business and receiving his pay. Forty black rats had been drawn from every hole and corner in the barn and threshing-floor, but only two brown ones—and they were quite young still—and no mice. But, as soon as the rat-catcher had gone, the old tom-cat died of sheer old age and laziness. He was buried in the garden with great pomp and ceremony. But, even before he was committed to the grave, Jens brought a young cat over from the keeper's; and there was every reason to hope that she was of a different sort from the old one.

The forester, it was true, said that she was the very image of what the old one was when she was young. And that too may have been right enough, for one can't judge youth by old age. This much, in any case, was certain, that she went hunting. The odd man had said that she must have her morning milk and nothing more before she caught a mouse or a rat. And so it stood. Whenever she showed herself for the first time, after her morning milk, she was asked:

"Where is your mouse or your rat?"

And gradually she grew so used to this that, as soon as she was asked, she ran off and fetched the mouse or the rat, which she had been careful not to eat before. Then, as a reward, she received a scrap of bacon, or something else that was left over from breakfast. But, on days when she had no mouse or rat to show, then she received no bacon either. That was as sure as March in Lent.

The young lady no longer interested herself in the matter, but left it all to the odd man. Whenever she caught sight of the hole in the dining-room wainscot, she sighed and said:

"You naughty, naughty Mouse, to abuse my trust in you so shamefully! I was good to you and gave you sugar every day; and you stole the cinnamon. Now I have been good to you again and taken away the poison which the rat-catcher put outside your hole. What advantage do you propose to take of me this time? But you can, if you like. I don't trouble about you now. I can't help you if the new cat gets hold of you some day: she is quite a different sort of cat from the old one and she will catch you yet, you'll see. It's your own fault."

When she talked like that, as she often did, it was hard for the little mouse to sit inside the wainscot and listen and not to be able to defend herself. She would so much have liked to tell her young lady that she was not quite so bad as she thought. She would so much have liked to have her little lumps of sugar again. For times were shocking, since the rat-catcher had been. She hardly dared eat a thing, for fear lest there should be a hidden poison in it. And she could hardly go anywhere, because of the new cat.

But she could not talk to the young lady. Nor did she dare venture across the barn. She would have liked to talk to her cousin from Copenhagen, but, one day when she went through the kitchen-drain, the new cat was sitting at the other end and was within an ace of eating her. So she had to be content with poor fare and a bad conscience.

Then, one morning, the house-mouse went out through the hole to the wood. It was at the time when the cat got her morning milk, so she thought there was a chance of peace and no danger. She ran a good way off over the snow, right to the foot of the big beech, where she knew that Cousin Wood-Mouse had her nest.

Then she squeaked three times in a particular manner which only mice understand and which means that they would like to talk to the individual concerned. And, when she had waited some time, sure enough the wood-mouse appeared:

"Good-morning, cousin," said the wood-mouse. "To what do I owe the honour of this visit? It is ages since I saw you last."

"Good-morning, cousin, and the same to you," said the house-mouse. "One doesn't go out for one's pleasure at this time of year."

"No, indeed, cousin," said the wood-mouse. "I always stay indoors, except just to take a mouthful of fresh air and throw out the shells. Look, here is my dust-heap."

Quite a little pile of nut-and acorn-shells lay outside the mouse-hole. The house-mouse looked at it and sighed:

"What a lot you've eaten already!" she said. "And I daresay you have a great deal more down there in your store-room."

"No, that I haven't!" said the wood-mouse. "I shall be glad if I can get through the rest of the winter on half-rations. If my own child were suffering want, I could not give it so much as a nut. Times are awfully bad."

"So they are," said the house-mouse. "My case is the same as yours. You need not fear, however, that I have come to beg. I have only come to have a chat with you. Can't we go into your place for a little while?"

The wood-mouse reflected a bit. She very much objected to having the other down and letting her see all the beautiful food that lay stored up below. So she shook her head with decision:

"Not so early in the morning, cousin," she said. "In an hour or two you will be welcome, if you dare go out then and risk meeting the cat. But the rooms haven't been done yet. I know how neat and particular you house-mice are, so I should be ashamed to show you my home before it's quite clean and tidy. I should prefer you to wait until the winter's over, when I have had my spring-cleaning."

"Oh, very well!" said the house-mouse. "Then we'll stay here, though it's horribly cold sitting on one's bare tail in the snow. As I said, I only wanted to talk to you a bit. It's about the family. I don't know if you have heard that a cousin of ours has arrived from Copenhagen?"

"No, I haven't," said the wood-mouse. "What's he called? Is he a smart fellow?"

"She's called the brown rat. It's a she," replied the house-mouse. "And she really was very smart at first. She came in the packing-case in which we get our groceries every year from the shop in Copenhagen. It is a great big case, full of the most delicious things you can think of. She had only found her way into it by mistake and so travelled across with it."

"That's what you may call travelling first-class," said the wood-mouse, laughing.

"One may indeed," said the house-mouse. "I should have no objection to travelling round the world in a packing-case like that. However, she was a young bride expecting her babies every day. She therefore at once made herself a home in the barn; and the children arrived four days after."

"Oh, yes!" said the wood-mouse. "There are always plenty of children and there are always more and more coming."

"That is so," said the house-mouse. "But now hear how things went. At first, Cousin Rat was extremely amiable. She treated me to sugar and cinnamon and flour and sugar-candy and so forth during the whole of the four days. You must know that she had gnawed herself out of the case, which stood in the barn waiting to be unpacked. Well, I accepted her invitation and ate away. Wouldn't you have done the same?"

"Certainly," said the wood-mouse. "One must never offend people by declining a kind offer. And when it happens to be a cousin ... and the goods are hers...."

"Well, they weren't exactly," said the house-mouse. "The case really belonged to the forester."

"According to that, nothing is ours," said the wood-mouse. "I work it out differently. I say that the mast and nuts out here are mine. And the larder in the forester's house is yours. And, in the same way, the case in which the rat arrived was hers. But go on and tell me how things went."

"Things went very badly," said the house-mouse. "For four days, we lived on the fat of the land. But, on the fifth, the young mistress and the man started unpacking."

"Oh!" said the wood-mouse. "Then the fun was over, I expect?"

"It was, cousin," said the house-mouse. "But that would have been all. Nothing lasts for ever in this world: not even a chest of groceries from Copenhagen, though it was the biggest I ever saw and simply bursting with good things. But, when they discovered that some one had been at it, they were angry; and we all got blamed for it, you see."

"And it was the rat who did it," said the wood-mouse. "That was really hard on you."

"So it was," said the house-mouse. "They would not believe it was the rats, because they had killed so many of them after the rats had bitten Jens' nose. And so it must be the mice: that went without saying. To judge by what I have heard them talk about since, the young mistress stood up for me as long as she could, but the forester and his man both said that, with mice and rats, it was six of one and half-a-dozen of the other."

"Yes, that's the worst of it," said the wood-mouse. "It's just as with me and the field-mouse. We have to suffer for our relations' misdeeds. Well ... and didn't your mistress find out how things stood?"

"She did not," said the wood-mouse. "Taken all round, things went about as badly as they could with me. You see, I had heard them say that the case was to be unpacked. And then there was some nice cinnamon, which I am so fond of. So, on the last night, I resolved to drag a piece over to my place, so as to have a bit to spare. I did so and managed to get it through the drain all right. But then it was so big that I had a difficulty in dragging it any farther. So I nibbled it into two pieces. One of these I got right down into my hole and the other just up to the hole. But then the door slammed and I was frightened and dropped the cinnamon and ran away."

"Well, you fetched it afterwards, I suppose?" asked the wood-mouse. "You said it was lying outside the hole."

"So it was," said the house-mouse. "But now I'll tell you how badly things went. When I got down into the hole, I fell asleep. I don't know how it is, but cinnamon always makes me so beautifully sleepy. And then I have the most wonderful dreams about bacon and the very nicest things I can think of. So I fell asleep and slept and slept and dreamt beautifully. When I awoke at last, it was broad daylight, as I saw the moment I put my nose outside the hole. The cinnamon was there all right. But the mistress was in the room, so I dared not take it. And, when she went out into the kitchen, she left the door open, a thing she never does as a rule. And, all the time, she was walking up and down. And then they began to unpack the case and she put the things away in the cupboard and the sideboard. And then she suddenly stopped in front of my hole, where the cinnamon was, you know, and then, of course, I was found out. She was very much distressed at my deceit, as she called it, and said that she had done with me and would never give me any more sugar. And, since that day, I have not had a single lump. It's a terrible loss to me."

"So it is," said the wood-mouse. "But what can you do? You can't explain the thing to her, you know."

"No," said the house-mouse. "I can't do that. And now the rat-catcher has been and a new cat has come, who is a regular demon at her business. It's a perfect miracle that I have escaped so far. I half wish I were dead. The good days in the forester's house are over; and they won't come back either. It's hard, when one was looking forward to having a fairly comfortable time in one's old age."

"Oh, you needn't think it's much better out here!" said the wood-mouse. "There's a new young forester come; and he's a terror!"

"I know," said the house-mouse. "He came down with the rat-catcher. Jens fetched them at the station."

"But the rat-catcher went back again," said the wood-mouse. "The young forester stayed here and is still here; and I don't expect he will ever go. He intends to grapple seriously with the mouse-plague, as he calls it, meaning the field-mouse. The mast and acorns are being gathered earlier than usual, so that we may starve to death. He wants to let cats loose in the woods, I heard him say. And owls are to be imported, as if there were not enough of them before! And foxes and martens and buzzards and polecats and ermines are to be preserved for five years. It will be a fine police-force."

"Yes," said the house-mouse, "there are bad times in store for all our family."

They sat for a while and idled, each wrapped in her sad reflections. The house-mouse felt horribly cold, because of her bare tail, and the wood-mouse wished her cousin would go away, so that she might run down to her warm nest.

"Tell me," said the wood-mouse. "How is our cousin from Copenhagen doing over in the barn? Haven't you talked to her?"

"No, I haven't," said the house-mouse. "She was particularly friendly when we had the packing-case: indeed, she even asked me down to see her rooms. But she warned me not to come over there otherwise. She said that I might run the risk of her eating me. She and some other brown rats once ate a kitten, she said. And I could see by the look on her face that it was true."

"Oh dear, oh dear!" said the wood-mouse. "But perhaps the rat-catcher or the new cat has caught her?"

"No," said the house-mouse. "She escaped; and so did most of her children. And they have multiplied in such a way that you simply can't turn for rats, Jens says."

"Then, you'll see, they will forget you all right," said the wood-mouse, "if only you are careful and discreet."

"Jens will forget me, perhaps," said the house-mouse, sadly. "But the mistress will never forget me, because she believes I deceived her. And the new cat has set eyes on my hole and she is on the look-out. Some day, sooner or later, I shall be eaten up."

"Yes, it's awfully sad," said the wood-mouse. "But what can one do...? Hullo, who's coming now?"

The house-mouse turned round and looked in the same direction as the wood-mouse. A black animal came running over the snow.

"I positively believe it is our cousin the black rat," said the house-mouse. "I didn't think there were any of them left. Yes, there's no doubt about it, it's the black rat."

"Good afternoon, cousin," said the wood-mouse and backed down into her hole until only her nose peeped out. "Welcome to the country. This is the first time, so far as I know, that I have had the pleasure of seeing you out here. You don't care much for nature, I believe."

"Give me food! Give me food!" screamed the black rat.

"I'm awfully sorry that you are hungry," said the wood-mouse. "Unfortunately I have just eaten my last nut. As you see, here's the shell. The house-mouse had been downstairs calling on me and can bear witness that there's not a bite or a sup to be found in my place."

She winked at the house-mouse to confirm the truth of her fib. But the house-mouse could not take her eyes off the black rat, who had lain down in the snow and was moaning piteously:

"You're catching cold, cousin," she said kindly. "You had better go back to the barn again. It's warmer there."

"I really don't care what becomes of me," said the rat. "To tell you the truth, it's all the same to me whether I die in one way or another. You say I ought to go back to the barn. That's where I've come from. There's no existing there for those loathsome rats from Copenhagen. They call themselves rats, but I don't believe that they are rats at all. I am sure they're a sort of fish by the way swim. And the way they eat! And the way they multiply! They have children once a week, I do believe. It's disgusting."

"It certainly is," said the wood-mouse. "Cousin House-Mouse and I were just sitting and talking about it, cousin. But what's to be done, cousin? I am hard pressed by the field-mouse and get the blame for all his villainy. Some time ago, the house-mouse had to put up with harm for your sake, because you bit the odd man in the nose or else ate and drank things. Now one has come who is stronger than you; and so it's your turn. Besides, it seems to me that you are big enough to send the rat home to where she came from."

"Big enough?" said the rat. "Big enough? That great brown brute is bigger than I am! And then there are so many of them! I am the last of my race. When I am dead, there will be no more black rats in this part of the country. And now I am going to die."

"Stop a bit! Cousin!" said the house-mouse. "Let us talk it over first!... Perhaps we can hit upon something or other!..."

But it was too late. The black rat stretched out her four legs and was dead and gone.

"Lord!" said the wood-mouse. "To think that she should go and die like that before our eyes! If you fall to the cat now and I to the owl and if the young forester destroys the field-mouse, then there won't be a single member of all our big family left."

"Yes, there will be: I'm here," said a deep, gruff voice close by.

"Gracious!" said the house-mouse and jumped right into the air. "There's the brown rat!"

And there he was. The brown rat stood and mumbled with his snout and sniffed at the dead black cousin, while keeping an eye upon the wood-mouse, who retreated a little farther still into her hole.

"Good-afternoon, cousin," said the wood-mouse. "Welcome to the country. I hope your outing will agree with you better than our black cousin's did with her. For she fell down and died where she lay."

"Cousin me no cousins!" said the brown rat. "It's awful the way you people out here in the country brag about relationship. What's become of the house-mouse?"

"She's run home," said the wood-mouse. "I believe she was afraid of you, which surprises me, for you look so good and kind."

"Thank you," said the brown rat. "I always appreciate a friendly word. I'm as hungry as the dickens. Have you something or other you can treat me to? I don't care what: I eat anything."

"Very sorry," said the wood-mouse. "Unfortunately, I have eaten up everything and have to starve myself for the remainder of the winter. The house-mouse got a couple of nuts out of me and the black rat the rest of my store. If you had come earlier, there would have been a morsel for you as well, perhaps."

"I think I will pay you a visit in your rooms," said the brown rat. "Or you can come up here for a bit and chat to me. I have never seen you, though we are cousins."

"Oh, we have become cousins now?" said the wood-mouse, laughing. "A little while ago, we were not. But thank you all the same. My hole, unfortunately, is too narrow for you to get through. And I don't feel equal to going out again to-day. I should catch my death of cold. As for my appearance, you have only to think of a pretty little, nice, fat mouse. Then you have me."

"Yes, if only I had you!" said the brown rat. "Then I should eat you straight away. But you are too clever for me."

Then he began to nibble at the dead black rat.

"What's this?" said the wood-mouse. "Are you eating your dead cousin?"

"Yes, I can't help her not being alive!" said the rat.

A little after, the black rat was gone, bones and all. The brown rat sat and licked his lips. Then he ran home to the forester's house.

The wood-mouse sat in her hole and thought it all over:

"Well, bless my soul, after all, what's the objection? The house-mouse will fall to the cat and I to the owl or the fox and the field-mouse to the young forester. Whereas the black rat has remained in the family."